The Chuparosa Chronicle Volume One

SHORT STORIES FEATURING THE DEANE WITCHES AND THEIR FRIENDS

By Vanessa Haney

Copyright © 2024 Vanessa Haney

All rights reserved.

Cover by Thomas Schroeder

ISBN: 978-1-963756-90-6

Dedication

To Laura Deane for being the big sister I never had, and to Sarah for allowing me to indulge my bratty side.

To my kindred spirit, Andrew Clarke: I hope you feel safe in the new family that I wrote for you, and I hope you know that they will never let you down.

Sebastian Scott, I love your big heart so much. I know you worry about losing her, but I promise that Laura will always be with you.

Finally, thank you to Brona, Fiona and Jaya. You bitches are helping me heal.

Also by Vanessa Haney

Heaven's Lost (Book 1)
Heaven's Watch (Book 2)
Heaven's Call (Book 3)
The Chuparosa Chronicle (Short Stories)
The Devil's Memories (Book 4)

Author's Note

The town of Chuparosa is home to plenty of adventures that for one reason or another just haven't found a place in my books. I created the Chronicle to make sure that they get the attention they deserve. The short story format allows me to expand on ideas that I loved but just couldn't fit anywhere else, and to experiment with other genres and styles while dragging my characters along for the ride.

The stories in the Chuparosa Chronicle tend to be more personal. They're full of Easter eggs and little details that have been great fun for me to write. Unedited versions of *Adam's Arrangement* and *Fire Resistance* used to be on my website, but this book contains their final forms along with seven more stories plucked from the population that shares its borders with the Other Side.

Heaven's Watch are always present but they're not the only ones who've had unusual experiences in town. So, if you're curious about their neighbors, I invite you take a peek through the blinds and read on...

Table of Contents

Welcome to Chuparosa!

If you are outdoorsy in Arizona, you probably hike countless hours across the state's vast mountain ranges. You encounter owls, snakes, spiders, javalina, rabbits, coyotes, and deer. You see the big cat paw prints in the sand and look around nervously for the mountain lion who left them.

But did you just catch something unusual out of the corner of your eye? *Surely that rabbit isn't three feet tall.* Did you see something that just doesn't make any sense? *Butterflies don't have teeth, do they?* You want to write it off because it's so hot and you know you didn't drink enough water. It could be dehydration making you feel as if the ground is tilted under your feet, but you have your doubts, don't you? Further investigation seems unwise, but you're drawn to this place even though it makes the hair stand up on your arms. If you've got an uneasy feeling inside telling you to get a move on, you may have stumbled into Chuparosa.

Chuparosa, Arizona sits at the foothills of a mountain range that taunts hikers with some of the most dangerous black diamond trails in the country. Some follow canyons with deep caves in their walls, some are lined with bizarre rock formations and some lead to waterfalls that gush in spite of the drought. Locals know that these anomalies are portals to the Other Side, but they try to leave well enough alone. It's not a good idea for residents of either Side to cross those boundaries. Keep in mind that the lines aren't always clear and not all the trails are marked.

It's a quiet place, until it's not. Most people don't move away and very few move in. Those who do have their reasons and though the town won't judge, it's got an energy so old that it can tell who belongs and who doesn't. Most outsiders are happy to get back on the outside but, since you're here, maybe you would like to stay a while. Hike the trails and meet the people who make Chuparosa their home. They are flawed but they are brave, and each one has a story to tell.

Adam Colter made his brief debut in Heaven's Lost, but I didn't know his whole story back then. It came together later when I was in the hospital with a bout of diverticulitis and unable to sleep. We had a trip to Bisbee planned for the following weekend and I insisted we go even though I was still recovering. Adam's entire backstory fell into place while we were there, so I don't regret any of that self-inflicted pain. It was on that trip that Cara became a point on my moral compass. Would I do what she did? I'm still not sure.

Adam's Arrangement

The pain stabbed low in Cara's left side all morning and what started as dull and uncomfortable became more frightening as the day wore on. Staring out of her office window at Tempe Town Lake, she frowned, wondering what hellish new ailment she would have to attend to.

Since turning fifty, her body found new ways to betray her almost daily. She likened the battle for her health to a twisted game of Whack-a-Mole with the elusive prize being a hundred-year birthday celebration. Whatever that was worth.

She took plenty of steps to get there on her own, inasmuch as she could control the aging process. The intrauterine device seemed to have curbed the frightening monthly blood baths, the statin she took was, in theory, drawing the *bad* cholesterol away from her artery walls, and the handful of supplements she choked down every morning should have been fighting off everything from thinning hair to Alzheimer's Disease.

So was the new pain something fatal, or just something she ate? While she contemplated how to deal with whatever was fussing around in her abdomen, her assistant's harried voice grew louder outside her office door.

"I don't think she's available, Mr. Kavanaugh." Jason was saying.

She turned from the window and rested her hand on the computer mouse, studying the screen in an attempt to look busy.

"She's always available for me." Lou Kavanaugh pushed open the door and marched in with Jason on his heels.

He stood in front of her desk but, not wanting to give Lou the impression that he was right, Cara didn't bother to look up. Though he was no one percenter, Lou was one of her biggest accounts and he would not allow her to ignore him. He stepped around the desk, grabbed her by the shoulders and kissed her on the cheek—a little too close to the corner of her mouth.

Jason blanched in horror. "Cara, I am so sorry."

"I can do this because I'm an old man." Lou bragged over his shoulder.

Jason, all of twenty-five years old, didn't realize that

Lou was right. Old men had been getting away with that shit since she bought her first shoulder-padded Casual Corner suit in the nineties. Unlike plenty of others she'd encountered in her career, Lou meant no real harm. It simply never occurred to him that she wouldn't want his shriveled lips anywhere near her. His inflated sense of self-worth had been fostered every day of his career.

She, on the other hand, was regularly reminded by her superiors that it was men like Lou, willing to take a chance on a woman, who ultimately gave her that office overlooking the lake.

She opened up Lou's account file and reflected on the real truth of his situation. Two years earlier, Lou learned that his former financial advisor had been robbing him blind with upselling and fees. Cara smiled at her computer, remembering the remarkable day they met.

It had started out miserably that morning when she discovered her new boyfriend was married. She'd just sent a direct message to his wife and popped an antibiotic to cure the urinary tract infection he'd given her when Lou entered her office and begged for her help.

She sipped cranberry juice while quietly untangling his funds from her competitor's automatic withdrawals and made more appropriate investments for a man of Lou's age and means. She rescued his micro-fortune, but he seemed to have forgotten about that over the years, preferring to dwell on the fact that it was because of him that she had earned a giant promotion.

Lou knew her value of course, but always framed the conversation in such a way that he looked like Cara's benefactor because his business benefited her career. In fact, he would have no business at all if it weren't for her. She seethed at this, but then there *was* that beautiful lake view.

She gave him a thin smile. "How's Leslie, Lou? Did she tell you that we had lunch the other day?"

At the mention of his wife, Lou moved from behind her desk and sat in the guest chair. Cara liked Leslie Kavanaugh very much. They were both career-oriented women of about the same age, which was roughly twenty years younger than Lou.

She indicated to Jason that he was free to go, but he was protective of his boss. He'd sensed that she wasn't feeling well and left the door ajar on his way out, ready to interrupt with a fake emergency in case Lou became particularly obnoxious. It was a blessedly short meeting though and when it was over, Cara gave Jason a list of instructions and left for the day.

Fearing the doctors would treat her like a hysterical woman, she sat in her car outside of the emergency room, almost convincing herself that she was in fact overreacting. The spasms only intensified though, so she gathered her resolve and forced herself to walk inside. The triage nurse took one look at her hunched posture and pale, damp skin, and lurched around the desk just in time for Cara to collapse into her arms.

"I have good news for you and, as always, some bad news too."

Dr. Emily Silas was genuinely cheerful, given that Cara hadn't presented with some sort of sexual assault or gunshot wound or both. When a woman collapses in the emergency room entryway with such dramatic flair, everyone gets worried. To Dr. Silas, a bout with diverticulitis was, while extremely painful for Cara, as good as it would probably get on the job that night.

"Diver…what?" By that time, Cara was sitting up—mostly—but tethered to a bag flowing with hydrating fluids and morphine.

"It's the kind of thing that happens when you reach a certain age." Dr. Silas gave her a knowing look over the top of her glasses. "But it can become life-threatening, so we need to keep you here for several days on intravenous antibiotics. Sit tight and I'll let you know when there's a bed available upstairs."

Cara picked up her phone and searched for 'diverticulitis'.

"Fabulous," she muttered to herself, "no more popcorn." It was her go-to dinner on busy nights but according to the medical journal she read, the likely culprit for the distress in her *colon of a certain age.*

She emailed Jason and her boss, not quite as panicked as she might have been a few years ago over missing a week of work. She was making mental plans to stay on top of her emails from the hospital bed when it occurred to her that she could not remember the last time she'd taken a sick day. What would it hurt to give an account manager a few of her cases? Dawn Travis was brilliant and would jump at the chance to help her out.

It would kill your career is what. Dawn Travis hasn't paid her dues yet. Are you just going to hand her a break like that?

Cara's invasive thoughts annoyed her. Dues? That was just a corporate way of saying that Dawn hadn't been shit on enough to get those cases. Maybe it was the medicine talking, but why not hand Dawn a break?

She leaned back on the gurney and let herself enjoy the feel of the morphine as it warmed her veins. For the first time in two days, Cara was not in pain.

Adam Colter stepped off the elevator onto the fifth floor of Desert Mercy Hospital, affixing a volunteer badge to his shirt. There was a chaotic shift change happening at the nurses' station, so he glanced furtively at a computer and smiled to himself. The floor was full that night and they would need his help.

He tried to volunteer in the hospital at least twice a week, but it was already Thursday and he doubted he could make it back before Monday. The explosion at the Chuparosa Sheriff's Station had been taking up a lot of his time.

Adam was the night supervisor at the utility company that shared the same small government building. He'd been sitting at his desk three nights earlier, arranging the next day's work sheets for his electrical crew when he heard the two officers arguing with third voice he didn't recognize.

He'd peered around the corner in time to see Deputy Sebastian Scott fire on what looked like an angel—wings and all. Fascinated, Adam lingered long enough to see the winged creature throw a fireball between Sebastian and Deputy Chuck Ruiz. The blast tossed him backward and knocked him senseless for several minutes.

When he recovered his wits, he saw Rueben Soto, the building's facilities director, helping Sebastian to his feet. Incredibly, no one was killed so he decided to let the situation play out, pretending he'd been on a job in the field before the *accident* was reported.

The parties involved appeared to appreciate Adam's investigative discretion, but it took time to craft the reports necessary to convince the powers that be to leave the case alone.

He would make it his business to learn the real story later because if there were angels in Chuparosa, Adam would like a word.

The hospital was not what he would call his *happy place*, but Adam felt more human there than anywhere else. He felt more connected to life on those floors, even the life closest to death. *Especially the life closest to death.* The people he encountered at the hospital were usually in their most desperate or most celebratory of hours and he found inspiration in their courage.

He poked his head in on Mrs. Carter who had been in and out for weeks battling a horrible case of bacterial pneumonia. Her husband snoozed uncomfortably in a chair by the window, so Adam brought him a warm blanket and a fresh pillow. The older man jumped when Adam touched his shoulder, then relaxed when he recognized the volunteer.

"Will these make you more comfortable?" Adam asked.

"Oh yes, thank you," Mr. Carter whispered. "Why do they keep it so damn cold in here?"

He covered himself with the warm blanket and nodded off again as Adam stood over his wife. The aura of death hung over her and the sticky sweet smell of it coated every inch of the room. The spirits in the place danced around her bed in anticipation of a newcomer to their realm. Adam brushed them aside and took her hand in his, but even he strained to feel the blood feebly pumping through her veins.

The night nurses chatted with him as he continued down the hallway, and he delighted in their banter. He could appreciate their dark sense of humor and marveled at how even the meanest of them would give everything in the fight to save a life.

Adam was outgoing and enjoyed being around people, but it was difficult for the nocturnal man. The life inside the clubs and bars he frequented wasn't real enough for him and though he loved his new job with the utility company, he hadn't made any close friends in town yet.

It was nice to be useful, even though his volunteer work was simple: fetch warm blankets, chat with nervous patients who couldn't sleep, get them ice, fix their televisions, and keep them from using the call buttons so the nurses could focus on more pressing matters.

Matters like the code blue in Mrs. Carter's room. Adam was two doors down when he felt the life leave her body and, as the professionals ran to her, he could sense the glee of the spirits throughout the place. He was unsure of the purity of their intentions, but in most cases did not fear those who were already dead. Every now and then, he envied them.

Making his way down the hall, he caught a wild collection of emotions and they were all coming from the same room. That was common enough, but the life force was so strong. Intrigued, he skipped the next two rooms and stood in the doorway of 517. A feverish woman slept fitfully, and Adam realized then that it was her dreams he'd been picking up on. He did not feel the heaviness of death in the room, but there were two spirits standing near the window. Sometimes they just liked to watch.

He entered a stolen password into the computer next to her bed and learned that Cara Marshall had a dangerous intestinal infection but was expected to recover with medication.

Her hair was a shade of blonde that he guessed cost her over three hundred dollars. Several strands fell across her face as she dozed and, in the dim light of the room, the expensive highlights cast a warm glow on her pale skin. He pushed the hair behind her ear and returned to her chart where he learned that she was fifty-one years old. About the same age he was when...

He jumped when she mumbled, "Someone just took my vital signs." Her voice was subdued from the pain medication, but her gray eyes were sharp and immediately suspicious of him.

"I'm a volunteer," he said quickly. "You were admitted late so I thought you might want a snack, but it says here you're on a liquid diet."

She made a pouty face. "Nothing but ice chips for me, I'm afraid."

He squeezed her hand. "I'll get you some."

In the hallway, he leaned the back of his head against the wall and wondered why he had touched her like that. What was wrong with him? Why had the warmth of her skin given him chills?

As he slipped away, she chastised herself for flirting with him. *Good god woman, you can barely sit up.* Blaming it on the drugs, she let her eyes flutter closed and by the time he returned with a cup full of ice, she was fast asleep.

He shooed the spirits away from the window and

watched for a while as the medication dripped into her arm. The nurse had missed a few times with the needle and Cara's vein was swollen from the trauma of the procedure. A small amount of blood oozed into the gauze around tube emitting a mellow, coppery scent. He followed the pulse through her body for several cycles before leaving the room in a panic.

Just before sunrise Adam walked the floor of his house followed closely by his dog, Carl. It was a manufactured home he'd designed especially for what he referred to privately as his *chronic condition*. There were only a few small windows and just one door to the outside. It wasn't unusual for someone who worked nights to black out their windows, not that the people of Chuparosa would find it weird in any case, but he disliked the isolation of that and opted for heavy curtains instead.

He was anxious, wondering how in the world he could see her again without coming off like a maniac. As the sun crept over the horizon, he pulled the thick curtain closed and crawled into bed. The craving was strong—he'd put it off for too many weeks—and it mingled with other needs that Cara Marshall had awakened in him that night.

He could ignore his desire, though the crisp, citrusy scent she wore and the feel of her soft curls between his fingers made his body ache. He could not ignore the way her sleepy smile played at the edges of his heart, out of nowhere poking at his loneliness as if it were a raw nerve. When he closed his eyes, he could still hear the sound of her breathing and of the blood coursing through her veins. Clutching a pillow, he turned over to his stomach and, just before sleep took him, Carl hopped up and curled protectively at the foot of the bed.

Feverish, but feeling a little better, Cara asked that they back off on the pain medication so she could do some work. Jason fetched her laptop from her car and a tote bag of necessities from her townhouse but wouldn't bring her a coffee from her favorite shop. She'd graduated from ice chips to a liquid diet, but he feared upsetting the charge nurse who terrified him.

She checked in with Dawn Travis and was not surprised to learn that the younger woman was off and running with the accounts she'd been given. Cara had been prepared to be resentful or possessive, but found she quite enjoyed the role of mentor. Pain and fever notwithstanding, she was also secretly enjoying her forced vacation. She wrote in her journal for the first time in months and found herself quietly daydreaming the hours away.

It was two nights before Adam returned and Cara was beginning to think she'd imagined her handsome ice chip man. She worked to suppress a girlish grin when he knocked softly on the door to her room. *Get. A. Grip.*

He held out a Starbucks cup. "It's late, so this is decaf. I heard that you keep asking for coffee and the nurse said it would be okay."

She reached greedily for the cup. "I'm not going to lie, the cafeteria here is a tragedy. This will be the best cup of decaf I've ever had, thank you."

They chatted pleasantly for a bit, and she studied him in the way she couldn't when she was so sick before. He looked to be about her age. He was taller than her, but shorter than most men she knew, maybe five-foot ten or so. His hair was dark brown and thick, cut short on the sides and a little longer on top, whisked carelessly into a side part. Adam had the body of a man who engaged every muscle, every day in a trade of some kind.

Since he wasn't shy, she learned that he was, in fact, an electrical engineer, working the night shift for a small-town utility company on the west side of Phoenix. He volunteered at the hospital on the east side of Phoenix simply because they would let him work after hours. There was the hint of an accent in his voice, but she couldn't place it and it was strongest when he mentioned his rescued dog, which was often.

"Your dog's name is…Carl?"

He chuckled. "I suppose it's unusual, but I once knew someone by that name who took good care of me the way my dog does."

In Maricopa County, one lived on the east side of Central Avenue or the west side, and it turned out they lived opposite each other.

"You've probably never heard of it before," he said. "It's a small place called Chuparosa. It wasn't even on a map until about twenty years ago." He laughed but was obviously proud of his little west side home and he didn't notice the slight gasp she made when he mentioned the name of the town.

In the hours just before dawn, when he could bear it no longer, Adam parked his pickup a few blocks away from an abandoned warehouse. Like any big city, there were dark corners in Phoenix where wicked things happened, and he'd gotten good at finding them. The dog fights occurred weekly and though the location varied, his heightened senses usually led him in the right direction.

The barking, snarling, and whimpering of the dogs, combined with the jeering of the small crowd made him sick. Creeping in the shadows outside, he remembered how he'd found Carl bloodied, chewed up, and left for dead in the middle of an abandoned arena. He tore the throat out of Carl's handler and that particular crime circuit had since become his favorite hunting ground. There were plenty of monsters to choose from and no one seemed to care if they disappeared.

With so few lights around the building it was easy for him to blend into the darkness, though, glancing at his watch, he drew an uneasy breath. He'd spent more time with Cara than he intended to so he couldn't be as picky as usual. He shook his head and vowed not think of her again in that place, preferring not to sully thoughts of his lovely new friend.

The monsters showed themselves quickly enough in the guise of two short, skinny men, one with a patchy beard, and the other bald with no facial hair at all. The bearded monster was carrying a small mutt under one arm while the other counted a wad of bills.

The bearded one grunted as he flipped the bloody bundle into a nearby trash bin, "There's money in those damn bait dogs but they sure don't last long."

Adam's eyes flashed with hot rage and he slid his tongue along his teeth, impatient for the perfect moment. The bald man handed the bearded one some cash and turned to leave. As he cleared the area, Adam struck out from his corner and grabbed the bearded man, dragging him by the throat to the alley.

As Adam's razor-sharp fangs slid into his jugular vein, he pushed the bearded man's scratchy jaw to an unnatural angle so as not to see the shock and agony on his face. His victim's expressions were a mirror of sorts that he'd long since learned to avoid. He had to work to control the retch from his belly as the blood flowed into his mouth and down his throat. He hated the taste of evil but gulped it down as one would a foul medicine.

Adam's body tingled as the monster's blood fed his brain and internal organs. Though he would often indulge in the self-loathing associated with one who must do something so unsavory to survive, he didn't pity the man dying from his bite nor did he pity himself, he just wished there were another way.

The man, delirious from the pain, gurgled and gasped, "Please, let me go and I'll get you a dog of your own. You can make some serious money." His pleas only reminded Adam that the difference between the two of them was that the monster had a choice, and he did not.

Fresh anger flowed through him, and he bit down harder, allowing himself to enjoy it. When the taste of blood shifted to what he likened with chewing on a piece of aluminum foil, Adam squeezed his fist and snapped the man's neck. Vitality and strength renewed, he wiped his chin with a bandana and flipped the dead monster over his shoulder into the bin, careful not to land him on top of the little dog.

Four weeks later, he sat outside with Cara at a small table on the patio as they finished up their dinner at her favorite Italian restaurant. She was feeling much better, but for the inability to eat nuts and popcorn for the rest of her life, and they had been on a handful of dates since her release from the hospital.

Cara took a sip of her wine and eyed him surreptitiously over the top of her glass. She'd selected the quiet location because there was a hard conversation they needed to have. Unsure if he would be ready for it, she had decided to take a chance since they weren't going to get any younger. She was already falling for him and it would not do to waste time and have to end things later over what she could only describe as ideological differences.

He squirmed a bit in his chair as she stared and, finally, she put down her glass and leaned over the bistro table. "What was your reason?"

His brows furrowed. "Reason?"

"Adam," she started carefully, "I should have told you before, but I grew up in Chuparosa. I was a year ahead of Laura Deane in high school. In fact, she's a client and I helped her start her business. In the eighties, our fathers were killed in a construction accident that took out most of the tradesman there. Rhonda Deschene used to read tarot cards for my mother."

She put her fingers to her temples as if she herself could not believe what she was about to say and lowered her voice. "I have *spoken* to a ground squirrel."

His mouth fell open as she continued, "You had to have moved to *that town* on purpose and I want to know your reason for doing so."

He'd been struggling all week with the selfishness of continuing their relationship. He knew their feelings for one another were mutual and growing stronger, but he'd not yet worked out his plan.

She ran her fingers across his forearm and rested her hand on top of his. "Adam?"

If she grew up in Chuparosa, she knew about the Other Side. Her mother might have even been a witch. *What if?* A familiarity with the weird things in town, even with the dangerous Deanes, could not prepare someone for a…for him. Her grip tightened on his hand and she cocked her head.

Finally, he met her gaze. "I want to tell you, but I don't want to do it here."

Something had changed in the register of his voice and alarm bells went off in her head. She moved her hand away from his and said, "I…I don't think I want to leave with you."

He knew then that it would probably end badly. He figured at best she would run from the restaurant and he would never see her again. But if she fainted, or if she screamed…

"I'm not going to hurt you, Cara. No matter what you feel next, please know that I will never hurt you."

His smile was warm and charming and though he was making her nervous, she couldn't help smiling back. Her smile faded away though, as his fangs lengthened in front of her. She gaped in disbelief for a moment, then jumped up, pushing her chair over behind her. He closed his mouth and covered his face with hands.

Their server came out to check on them and glared at Adam while righting the chair. Cara was trembling but her voice was steady. "I'm alright. I thought I saw something, but I didn't."

When they were alone again, he said, "You saw it Cara, but remember my promise."

She remained standing next to her chair, and said quietly, "You said you wouldn't hurt me, but that was a lie."

It was then that he realized she wasn't trembling with fear, she was trembling with fury.

She considered how happy she'd allowed herself to be since her stay in the hospital. She had re-evaluated so much and was truly enjoying her more relaxed lifestyle and her new love. Just then it all seemed so stupid. *New love?* She was not twenty-two years old, and she had known better, and she was ashamed.

She balled her fists and glared at him. "What were you thinking? Since I've had the audacity to exist past my 'sell by' date that I would jump at the chance to be a blood tap for you? Or am I just a temporary salve for your loneliness?" She looked to the ceiling. "I let you into my house. God Adam, I let you into my bed."

He stood and pulled out her chair. "If you won't leave with me, please sit down for a minute." She did but flinched away when he put his hand on her back.

He gritted his teeth and sat down hard. "I'm capable of finding a temporary salve to sleep with, if that's what you mean. He rolled his eyes. "But you're right, I am lonely, and I wasn't thinking anything, I was hoping."

She looked down at her hands and didn't say anything for several minutes. Evenutally, he shoved some twenties in the server book and rose to leave. "Do what you want, but we connected on a deeper level and you can't tell me I'm wrong."

Alone at the table, she found herself embarrassed over her reaction, and then angry about being embarrassed, and then she laughed out loud. A god damned vampire stormed out on her because she hurt *his* feelings. Then, her eyes reddened as she realized she'd also hurt her own feelings by letting him leave. As another realization hit her, she kicked the table leg in frustration and pulled out her phone to order a rideshare.

Adam slammed the door to his pickup and laughed bitterly to himself, "Well, she didn't run away."

He expected her to be afraid, not pissed off and offended. He had been prepared to console her and perhaps explain his *condition*, not to get defensive and fight about it.

He spotted her walking out of the restaurant, checking her phone, and looking around. Then he slapped his hand to his forehead and got out of the truck.

Taking a deep breath, he trudged over to her. "Cara, I was angry and I forgot that I drove us here. Please let me take you home."

She glared at him, but her eyes were wet with tears that hadn't fallen yet, and he thought for a moment that she might leave with him after all. He desperately wanted to try their conversation again, but then her ride pulled up and she turned on her heel, climbing in the back seat without saying a word.

He drove back to Chuparosa feeling like an idiot. He hadn't been honest with her about what he wanted, and she knew it. It was true that he was falling for her, but he didn't want another mortal relationship. He'd lived through that pain before and learned that love was never going to be enough for him. He wanted a companion for life—his life. Her practical nature, education, experience, patience, and yes, her age had factored into his choice. It wasn't fair, but he'd hoped that her slightly jaded outlook and sensitivity about getting older, particularly after her health scare, might convince her to join him.

On his way home, he spotted some lights flickering at the YMCA. Pastor Andrew Clarke's 4Runner was parked outside next to Deputy Scott's truck. *What were they up to so late?* He picked up Carl at the house and headed back to the gym.

Pushing open the main door, he followed the muffled sounds of music to the community room in the back of the facility. That room was used for after school programs, but Pastor Clarke had permission to conduct his services there on Sundays. The pastor was also allowed to use the space for other meetings of importance to Chuparosa, mainly Alcoholics Anonymous. When Adam opened that door, his senses were overwhelmed by the sound of Judas Priest filling the air from a small, beat-up boom box the other men had balanced on top of a pile of folding chairs.

Bash was on a ladder with a drill and Drew was unboxing some light fixtures. As they worked, their heads bobbed almost imperceptibly to the heavy metal music. They had cut the electricity and were using battery powered lamplight, which explained the flickering he'd seen from outside. Adam waved his hand in the Preacher's peripheral vision to get his attention without startling him. Drew nodded a greeting and turned down the music.

Bash stepped off the ladder and reached out to shake Adam's hand, jumping back a bit when he noticed the enormous, one eyed, brindle Pitbull terrier standing there with his spotted tongue hanging out.

"What the hell is that?"

Adam raised an eyebrow. "That is Carl."

"Jesus." It was the most hideous dog Bash had ever seen. "What happened to him?"

"I took him in after he was injured in an illegal fight."

Drew's stomach turned. "I thought those poor dogs had to be put down if they were fighters." He cautiously stuck his hand out for Carl to sniff. "This one doesn't seem like such a bad guy though."

Adam leveled his gaze on Drew. "The bad guy *was* put down."

Bash wrestled briefly with his law enforcement side, swallowed hard, and mentally filed the information. He didn't know Adam Colter well, but that would have to change.

"Anyway," Adam continued, "I saw the lamps and wondered if you could use a hand."

Bash put his hands on his hips. "Are you working Saturday nights now too?"

"No." Adam scowled at the ground. "I was on my way home from a date that did not go as planned."

Bash grinned. "Are you saying that there was a fight, a supernatural event, or that you didn't get laid?"

Adam poked around in one of the boxes. "Yes."

The other men nodded sympathetically, but Bash couldn't help himself. "Was Carl there, by any chance?" That ugly beast wasn't going to help any man's game.

Drew handed Adam the extra drill. "We're doing a favor and swapping out the track lighting for the director of the Y. He doesn't want to disrupt daily activities with the work."

Adam sneered. "You mean he doesn't want to pay a proper contract, so he's taking advantage of your skills and your good nature."

The others nodded and Bash reclimbed the ladder to continue taking down the old lighting. Adam wasn't particularly fond of Judas Priest, but they seemed to enjoy it well enough, so he reached over and turned up the volume before climbing the other ladder with his drill.

Drew smiled in appreciation. At seventeen years old, one of the worst beatings he'd ever received from his strict, evangelical father was after sneaking off to a Judas Priest concert. If the old man had only known that his son lost his virginity that night as well, he would have simply passed away from the horror of it all. Drew squirmed under his shirt, suddenly conscious of the nasty scars that his father's belt left on his back but, despite the cruel punishment, it had been one of the greatest nights of his life.

When the work was done and the power restored, Drew reached into a small cooler next to his toolbox and handed each of them a beer. "Thanks for your help."

They sat in silence for a few minutes admiring the new lights and enjoying the beer, then Bash began to gather the packaging to stuff it back in the boxes.

"It sucks that you had a crappy night," he said, "but things went a lot faster once you showed up."

"Well, it's my own fault," Adam admitted.

"Usually is," Bash said, breaking down a box with the heel of his boot.

Adam's lips thinned. "She's a grown woman with a life of her own and I should have known better."

"Older women will rock your world," Drew mused cheerfully, recalling again the Judas Priest concert. "Do you mind me asking what happened?"

Adam shrugged. "I'd like to take things to the next level, but I went about it the wrong way. I'm not even sure I can protect her out here." He waved his hand at the window and the darkness of Chuparosa.

"A good friend of mine once told me that women like that don't want protectors, they want partners."

Bash smirked at Drew's reference to his advice and dragged the box to the bin outside. Adam took note of the way the deputy favored his left side, and that there were gashes and bruises in various stages of healing on both men. The explosion and their subsequent battle in the desert hadn't been that long ago.

It was Adam's understanding that they fought that night against the very powers of hell and Rueben Soto had lost his life in the effort. The two amiable fellows he'd worked the hours away with were, in fact, dangerous men who carried heavy burdens with nothing like Adam's strength to help them.

When Bash returned, Adam asked, "Was it an angel?"

The Deputy's eyes turned cold and he moved shoulder to shoulder with the Preacher, whose own features had abruptly hardened. The battle bonded closing of their ranks answered Adam's question, so he said softly, "That's all I needed to know."

Drew slammed the lid on the toolbox. "Don't go looking. I promise you won't like what you find and we don't need that shit right now."

"You misunderstand." Adam squared up his shoulders. "I have certain, um, abilities. Just know that you can call on me in the future, if necessary."

Bash shot Drew a look and grabbed a second beer from the cooler. "What can you do?"

Adam's cell phone alerted him just then with a text notification and he gave the others a crooked smile. "This will have to wait because I have been asked to present my case. But please remember my offer."

A mischievous glint flickered in Bash's eyes, and he rubbed at his beard. "They say when you're making a presentation, it helps to imagine your audience naked."

Adam coughed. "I'm afraid that would be the opposite of helpful right now."

Cara stared at her phone in disbelief. She had furiously typed out the text and sent it without even taking a breath: I want to know everything.

She tossed the phone on the couch as if it had bitten her, and then stomped around her townhouse. How dare he? She wasn't really surprised to learn he was a vampire. That part of the conversation was only upsetting in the sense that it complicated their relationship. Given how she spent her childhood, he could have told her he was the Javelina God, and she would not have batted an eyelash. In Chuparosa, you wouldn't necessarily judge someone for being a vampire. You would, however, judge him for not hiring a lawn guy to keep the bushes under control while he slept during the day.

He'd fed her that line about their deep connection, but the subtext was clear. He was looking for someone to go the distance with him. A long, long distance. He assumed that she would jump at the chance for immortality, that she would give up her hard-earned lifestyle and run away to that small town. She poured herself a glass of wine and popped three Ibuprofen in her mouth.

What angered her even more was that his demented version of a Hallmark Christmas movie was sounding better the more she thought about it. Since her first hot flash, she'd been raging against the unwelcome transformation of her body. And there she was, unexpectedly faced with the opportunity to stop time and seriously considering it. She put the wine glass to her forehead. *Am I insane?*

Her feminist sensibilities bristled at the notion of giving up so much. Then she thought about another twenty or so years of Lou Kavanaghs and married losers, and realized there was actually quite a bit that she would give up. In a heartbeat. Adam had no doubt suffered unimaginable losses over time and just wanted a more permanent arrangement. She tucked her feet underneath her on the couch and closed her eyes, remembering the tenderness of his touch. She had to admit that he was offering her a lot more than perpetual Botox, but forever really meant *forever* with a man like him.

That they truly cared for each other was quite a bonus and she sat with that thought for a long time. If she decided not to do it, he would end their relationship and she couldn't blame him. What would be the point of going on? Her heart would be broken, and she could not play with his by changing her mind. She blinked, and a tear that had been clinging to her lashes escaped down her cheek. Her phone remained quiet, and she feared that it was he who had changed his mind.

Studying the red wine in her glass, she realized there was no getting around the uglier terms of the deal. She knew exactly what vampires had to do to survive. Could she do that? Would she try to do noble things with the power she would be given? Did she even want to? How did he make it work for himself? What would Gloria Steinem do?

She'd been so wrapped up in her thoughts that when her phone buzzed, the sensation nearly scared her to death. The text was from him but there was no message, only an address.

Driving through one's hometown after being away for many years takes an odd toll on a person. Cara had no harsh feelings about Chuparosa. She often missed it when she spoke to Laura Deane on the phone, but the experience added to her anticipation and she was loaded with emotion when she pulled her car in front of Adam's house.

Unsure of what to expect, she'd dressed casually in leggings, a hooded sweatshirt and tennis shoes. She'd tried to prepare for anything, even to run.

He opened the door, dressed casually himself. Barefoot, in a pair of jeans and a blue flannel shirt with the top buttons undone. She caught his woodsy scent as he ushered her in and sighed as she brushed against his solid form in the doorway. *Merciless man.*

Carl approached, sniffing at her legs and the dog moved protectively in front of Adam when she jumped back in alarm.

Adam stepped in between, holding out his hands to both of them. "This is Carl. Carl, be nice."

"Hello Carl." She did her best to relax and regain her composure and was overcome by compassion when she paused to study Carl's one-eyed face. "I heard you're a good boy, looking after our Adam."

Carl eyed her doubtfully and stood on guard as they sat down at the kitchen table. Adam's house was austere on the outside, and gardening was probably never on his agenda, but she was taken aback by how pleasant and homey it was inside. He'd installed hard wood floors, and antique rugs stretched across every room. The furniture was also antique, but practical. They sat at a pine wood table that had been oiled over time to a near glossy finish. The obviously modern items in the home were his couch and television, but she'd never met anyone who didn't upgrade those comforts whenever possible. His laptop was closed and charging on the kitchen counter, upon which she noted there was also a toaster, but no microwave.

He was quiet while she took everything in and after a few moments she folded her hands and met his eyes.

"Let's start with your age."

He'd already searched his memories for the best place to begin. "What really matters is that I was working as a miner in Bisbee when I was attacked by a vampire. That was in 1899."

She gasped aloud. For some reason, she'd assumed he would be ancient and have wild tales about a life far away that she couldn't possibly understand; but she'd been to Bisbee, Arizona at least a dozen times and knew its mining history well.

He stood, and from a drawer behind him handed her a chunk of raw copper which was roughly the size of a sticky note pad. She turned it over in her hands and twisted in her chair to watch him as he padded through the house telling his story. An infectious fever had taken hold of many of the miners in his camp and back then, even in his early fifties, he was an old man quite susceptible to such things.

He spoke to her from something like a dream state, telling her things she gathered he'd not said out loud in ages. He was affable and outgoing before the fever but had somehow managed to make and enemy of a German miner named Walter. Walter came to his sick bed one night and tore at his throat until Adam begged for death.

"You do not get to die." Walter had said.

Adam couldn't remember drinking Walter's blood, but it didn't matter because he had been changed forever after that.

He plopped down on the couch with his head in his hands and she moved next to him, raking her fingers through his hair.

"You don't have to go on."

He shook his head and continued anyway, "My good friend Karl said he was Walter's brother. I know now that he was his thrall."

"Thrall?"

"You referred to it as a 'blood tap'."

She gagged. "Oh."

"Karl looked after me in the early days and taught me everything he could before…" His voice trailed off and she could guess how well Karl's kindness went over with Walter, so she shifted Adam's focus for him.

"Tell me how it works—dispel the myths for me."

"I'm not dead, Cara. I'm immortal and it was done to me. It was an excruciating violation of my humanity that has come with a terrible price. It's true, I could go to sleep outside tonight and wake up in flames with the sunrise, but I'm not suicidal."

He stood up again, his voice thick with emotion as he continued, "After all these years, I'm still angry and I have questions that I may never get to ask."

He had thought for a while that if there were angels about, he might corner one of them for answers. But after working with Bash and Drew that night, he found he was more interested in fostering friendships with them than seeking out what was likely to be just another source of pain.

The table seemed more official to him, so he took her hand and led her back to her seat. "I never should have approached you in the hospital, but you were right and I'm tired of being alone. I made sure you wanted me before I ever touched you, but do you understand the level of consent required to make a vampire? I've never even considered it until now."

Perhaps because she was so tired, the absurdity of that statement struck her as comical and she giggled out loud, covering her mouth with her hand.

He chuckled himself but said sadly, "If it weren't such an awful choice..."

"Tell me more," she pressed.

"I can eat and drink like anyone else, but I do need blood to survive."

It thrilled her ridiculously to know that she would not have to give up cheese. "Where do you get the blood?" It could not be Chuparosa, and the hospital would be too terrible. She looked around the room for clues until her eyes settled on poor Carl. "You're a vigilante."

He didn't argue with her, so a related thought crossed her mind. "How do you get into those places?"

"A business is just a building, and I can enter them freely, but I can't go into a home where I'm not welcome. I didn't mean you any harm, but I should have told you before you let me in." A troubled shadow crossed his face as he remembered the countless occasions in which he cavalierly accepted the invitations of people who weren't aware of the potential danger they were in. "A home pulses with life, growing with its owners and reflecting their values. People should feel safe at home."

"Do you have a reflection in a mirror?"

He shrugged. "Unless the mirror is cursed."

She was a little disappointed for him, but perhaps it was more of a female fantasy to never again have to obsess over her appearance.

"Before you ask why I stayed in Arizona," he said, rubbing his forehead, "with the right precautions I *can* venture outside in the daytime, but I rarely find it worth the risk."

She looked up in astonishment. "You took that risk after our first night together."

She could tell he was tired of talking and the sun was rising, making him vulnerable. In the end, she supposed he'd taken as a big a chance having her there as she had in showing up. How far was each of them willing to go?

"Let's sleep on it," she said.

He led her to his bedroom and that's what they did, with Cara snuggled into his chest and Carl grudgingly curled at their feet. It was a scene he wanted to repeat forever, but it was no surprise that when he woke up, she was gone.

A note on the nightstand read: *I love you, but I don't know if I can do it.*

Two months later, Adam stood gazing at the sunset from the safety of his kitchen with the taste of her still fresh in his mind. Her blood was sweet and fiery like a hard ginger candy melting on his tongue, and it genuinely saddened him that he would never experience it again. He'd worked hard to burn the memory of that extraordinary night into his brain.

Cara was an early riser and he found her in the guestroom tapping away at her laptop with Carl resting at her feet. She'd started a small financial consulting business of her own and hand-picked a few clients who were more than willing to follow her from the bank. Lou Kavanaugh was not among her selections.

She smiled up at Adam, offering a drink from a wine glass on the desk. Still a bit squeamish about her new dietary requirements, she'd taken to mixing blood with Bordeaux.

"Did I wake you?" she asked.

He shook his head and, curling his lip, took the glass from her hand. It wasn't as bad as he'd expected it to be and her concoction would make a useful substitute to have on hand. He could not foresee the future but, for the time being, Adam's arrangement with Cara appeared to be working out.

"Look what I found."

He peered over her shoulder at a news article on the screen. The headline read: 'Admitted Rapist Freed on Bail Disappears in Phoenix.'

She looked into his eyes and announced, "I think I

can do it this time."

He rested his hands on her shoulders and gave them a squeeze. "Then, we'll find him."

Adam's phone rang and he looked from the small screen to Cara. "Something must be wrong."

When he answered, Drew Clarke's voice was grave.

"Can you come to Laura Deane's house?"

Adam clenched his jaw. "Is she okay? What do you need?"

"No, she's not. Bring a generator…and those abilities you were talking about."

I grew up very near Perryville Prison and on occasion escapees would hide out in my elementary school. I never met one, but my young imagination went bananas with the possibilities. These days, the idea of running into an escaped prisoner is way less exciting. In fact, that sort of thing routinely finds its way into my nightmares. Even so, I think Rhonda and Audi do a good job of mixing fear with fun while bringing to life this variation of a story that my twelve-year-old self came up with.

The Prisoner Exchange

Kyle flopped onto his backside and slid down the embankment. The wash was still crowded with debris from the summer's flash floods and he had to dive away to avoid landing on a dead Saguaro at the bottom.

He'd been running for what seemed like hours and though his breath came in ragged gasps, he could not spare a single second to rest. The muscles in his legs burned and tiny pebbles worked their way into his socks as he slogged through the deep sand. Even so, he welcomed the landscape that would give him cover for miles.

He looked up without slowing and smiled to himself. The mountains were getting closer, which meant it would only be a couple of hours before the exchange. He'd studied that mountain range for months from his cell and would soon make one of its many caves his temporary home. He would first trade his thin vinyl mattress for a dirt floor, then he would slip into town, ditching loneliness for a woman with a car. Finally, he would drive south, swapping his country for Mexico, and the prisoner exchange would be complete.

Kyle knew the plan was a bit shaky, but he'd made it so far, and if at any point things went haywire, he would go out with guns blazing like Butch Cassidy. Maybe his new woman, whoever she was, would have a gun too.

While scanning the mountains for evidence of one of the caves, he caught his foot in between the branches of a felled tree. His knees hit first, and his arms could not fully extend before his face smacked on to the coarse sand, which tore against his skin like a cheese grater. He groaned and pressed up to find himself nose to nose with an enormous jackrabbit.

"What the fuck?" He yelped and scrambled away until his back was pressed against the shallow canyon wall. He squeezed his eyes shut, convinced a brain injury was causing hallucinations, but when he opened them, the rabbit was still there, unmoving and watching him curiously. It had to be at least three feet tall, not counting its ears. Kyle had never seen such a thing, but he was fairly new to Arizona and, it was the wild west, after all.

A rattlesnake as long as a baseball bat had once

made its way into the prison yard, so maybe all of the wildlife was huge and no one who lived there made a big deal about it.

His stomach rumbled and it occurred to him that a pizza would have been preferable, but if the stupid rabbit was just going to stand there, he could turn it into a housewarming dinner in his new cave. He spit out some sand and shifted his weight, slowly raising himself to his knees. The rabbit seemed unfazed so he lunged for it, but just before his hands wrapped around its neck, the beast opened its mouth into a wide grin revealing three rows of razor-sharp teeth.

Once again, Kyle dove sideways, but that time grabbed tightly to a dead cactus, ignoring the spines that dug into his palms as he used it to clamber up the embankment.

From the top, he peered down as the rabbit bounded away and disappeared in the bushes. Kyle doubled over with his hands on his knees, laughing to himself as if maybe it hadn't been real. He had come upon a dirt road with one house at each end and was anxious to get out of sight, but also starving. He trotted toward the farthest one, chosen only for the orange tree in the front yard.

In the back yard, Audra Deane twisted a lemon off its branch and held it to her nose. Rhonda's lemons were the best in town and Audi smiled at her as the bright, uplifting aroma filled her senses. Rhonda DeSchene had been a friend to the Deane women since Audi's mother, Sarah, was a teenager. She'd helped the witches develop their powers and acted as a surrogate mother when

Audi's grandmother abandoned the role.

No other relationship in their lives mattered more and the reverence with which the Deanes treated her often confused Rhonda. She'd simply opened her door to them, but they would argue what was behind that door was more magical than they could ever hope to be.

She was grateful for Audi's devotion that day though because as she began to move more slowly with age, picking lemons had become one of her most painful chores. She steadied the ladder as Audi descended and then surveyed their harvest. Three wicker baskets teemed with lemons and she nodded approvingly at the girl. They would do well at the Full Moon Farmer's Market on Saturday.

Audi's smile faded as her feet touched the ground. For a split second, she saw Rhonda lying in a bed, pale and gray, with blood seeping through her gown. Then, just as quickly as it had come on, the vision faded and the older woman stood in front of her again, her head tilted with concern. The vision so rattled Audi that she sat down hard on a lawn chair, covering her mouth with her hands.

"What's the matter with you, girl? Don't act like you've seen a ghost around here or I'll get out the sage right now."

Audi shook her head, laughing. Then she lied, "It's nothing, I'm just dizzy after being on the ladder."

"Have you taken a pregnancy test lately?" Audi had told her earlier of another vision she'd had of her and Noah's baby, but she decided to keep the newest vision to herself.

Kyle peeled an orange and studied the house from the edge of the yard. There were two cars in the driveway, but he shaded his eyes with his hand and saw no one when he looked through the picture window. He popped the last orange section in his mouth, tossed the peel on the ground and tried the door. Smiling to himself when it opened—*small town trust*—he snuck inside for a look around. The lights were out, but he noticed candles burning everywhere as he traveled through the house.

"Romantic," He said under his breath and made his way to the bedroom. He'd thought he would wait there, but something unexplainable kept him out of Rhonda's private space. Overwhelmed by feelings he could not explain, he turned away from the bedroom door and clicked on a lamp in the living room. Rummaging through the drawer of an end table, he found her little .38 pistol.

"Nice," he said and slipped it into the waistband of his pants.

Outside, a hot wind whipped their hair across their faces, but the women shuddered from a chill and noted that the leaves on the trees didn't move. Rhonda's wards were strong, yet they trembled and shook, warning them of trouble inside. They exchanged looks and turned to the house.

"What now?" Audi asked.

They expected perhaps another angel, something sinister that escaped from Hell, or maybe a creature on the prowl from the Other Side. That a dangerous human had broken into the house never once occurred to them.

From the kitchen, Kyle spotted the two women on

the back porch. They turned in slow circles but did not see him through the window. He figured the younger one to be around twenty-one years old and he let his gaze travel slowly up her legs to the long brown curls blowing around her head. Her large brown eyes projected suspicion as they searched for whatever it was that they were looking for but, in his mind, those eyes would soon be begging him to let her live.

A person could speak volumes with their eyes, especially if they couldn't speak with their mouths. In fact, he would never bother with the rest of it if it weren't for the eyes. He kept them too, as little reminders of their private conversations.

A pickup was parked out back and, while he didn't want to get too cocky, he couldn't help but feel as though fate had led him to the little house in the desert where all of his needs were somehow met. He even smelled something delicious cooking on the stove. His mouth watered, but the older woman was stepping up to the porch, and even though the younger one tried to stop her she turned the knob.

His eyes darted around for a place to hide and then he quickly squeezed himself into a large armoire near the fireplace. The shock in their eyes when he jumped out would be priceless.

Billy Tate sighed with relief as Sheriff's Deputies Chuck Ruiz and Sebastian Scott returned to the station early after a mountain patrol on horseback. Though they were grateful not to have come across anything suspicious, they were hot and tired.

"God damn," Bash complained while he hung up

his cowboy hat, "I think it's gonna be an early sum—".

Billy, who minded the front desk in those days, wore a grim expression that stopped him mid-sentence.

"You'll wanna look at this," he said, handing them an email he'd printed moments earlier.

When Chuck looked up from the page, Billy added, "The Department of Corrections has got troopers spread out from Buckeye to Avondale but no one's coming to Chuparosa. I called Don and he said they figure the rough terrain around here will dissuade him."

"Are you fucking kidding me?" Bash took out his phone and pressed the contact for 'Don at DOC'. After Don repeated what the email said, he asked Bash to put him on speaker mode.

"Listen," he warned, "this guy is violent and unhinged and home invasion is his thing. Torture."

"Christ," Chuck groaned.

"The Marshal's office will check in with you, but they're stretched thin, and I know you've got *other* means at your disposal." Don was from Chuparosa, and he knew that they knew exactly what he was talking about.

"Should it become necessary, don't hesitate to use them."

The energy in the house grew heavy around Audi and Rhonda as soon as they walked in. Again, they looked at each other and Audi gave an almost imperceptible nod toward the door, just slightly ajar, and an altar cloth that had fallen out of the armoire when Kyle climbed in.

Rhonda took Audi's hand and said, "Dinner is

almost ready."

Kyle was hiding in the cabinet that contained most of her more advanced spell supplies, but there was almost nothing they couldn't do with the kitchen spice rack. While she made her selections, Audi took a little cactus from the windowsill and dropped it in the pot. Rhonda added cayenne pepper, garlic, black mustard seed and mullein while Audi whispered the most violent words she had ever spoken over the pot.

The soup's aroma wafted into the cabinet and Kyle could take it no more. He jumped out, expecting his all-time favorite look from the women: the startled look of confusion just before the realization that something awful was about to happen. But Audi's eyes were fierce, and she raised her hands, using her power to throw him backward. He bounced off the armoire but recovered quickly, firing the gun.

Rhonda crumpled at Audi's feet and as she knelt beside her Kyle pressed the gun to her temple. He positioned himself in front of the young girl, waiting to see the terror in her eyes, but again she surprised him. He didn't know how important Rhonda was to her and he didn't know that he wasn't the first person to put a gun to her head. So, what he saw in her eyes was not terror. It was pure rage.

He nearly flinched away, but his stomach growled with hunger, and he ordered her to get him some soup. Keeping the gun on her, he sat down at the table while she ladled a small amount into a bowl. He motioned with the gun for her to add more, so she filled the bowl and slammed it on the table in front of him. He jumped up when some of the hot liquid sloshed into his lap and shoved her down in the seat across from him.

"You'd better watch yourself." He kept the gun on her with one hand and shoveled spoonful after spoonful in his mouth without even tasting it. After a while, he looked up and said, "I almost killed a rabbit for dinner, but the rabbits around here aren't right, they got some kind of sickness."

"Chuparosa would never let itself get used by scum like you," she scoffed.

He had no idea what she was talking about but since his belly was full, he decided that he would make her scream a little and then they would take the truck out back and head to Mexico.

They had no sooner hung up with Don when Laura Deane called.

"Bash, we can't get in touch with Rhonda," she said.

He heard Sarah in the background say, "Audi went over there to help her pick lemons and neither one of them is answering." She was trying unsuccessfully to keep the panic out of her voice. "Rhonda hasn't been feeling well lately, so can you meet us there in case she needs extra help?"

"Rhonda's not answering," he told Chuck.

"Aw shit, man." Chuck's jaw tightened, "Her house is closest to the highway."

"Laura, listen to me baby," Bash said, "you two stay away from her house. We'll go."

"What do you know, Bash?"

"Look, a prisoner escaped, and he might be—"

"Oh my god, we'll meet you there."

"No! Laura wait!" But she had ended the call.

"Damn stubborn woman," Bash growled and

grabbed his hat, running out the door with Chuck on his heels.

Chuck turned the key in his ancient county issued truck and whispered a short prayer, but it wouldn't start. He slammed his fist into the steering wheel and muttered, "Fuck me."

Kyle jerked Audi up by the arm, and with the gun in her back, nudged her toward the bedroom. Just past the armoire, he released her and moved his hand over his stomach. A wave of dizziness washed over him, and he fell against the wall. Audi began to mumble, and with each word his pain intensified.

"Shut up, you crazy—" He doubled over, a sheen of sweat covering his body. "What did you do to me?"

She took a step back and swept her hands in front of her using her power to throw him against the front door. She took her phone from her back pocket and called for help as he curled up in the fetal position.

"Are you okay?" Billy blurted when he answered her call.

"I'm fine," she said, picking up the gun and kneeling by Rhonda's still body, "but I need an ambulance at Rhonda's house."

"Chuck and Bash are on their way in Bash's truck."

She glanced at Kyle twitching on the floor. "They don't have to rush, but I need that ambulance right now."

She pressed a clean dish towel over Rhonda's gunshot wound while Kyle tried to throw up. She waved a hand in his direction without looking up and the vile soup caught in his throat went back down. He writhed around for a bit and then after a few tries, managed to inch over to the front door.

"I'm not going back to prison, you stupid bitch."

She smiled at him and said, "No, you're not."

Audi followed him as he crawled outside and then she snatched up a passing tumbleweed. She'd never used such baneful magic before but as she thought of losing Rhonda, her intentions were stronger than ever and crystal clear. She hurled the tumbleweed at Kyle and went back inside, closing the door behind her.

Tumbleweed thorns clung to Kyle's clothes and dug into his skin. They grew into long vines that curled around his limbs and his neck, enclosing him in a ball of natural barbed wire. He opened his mouth to scream, but all that came out were gurgles and wretches as the thorny strands pushed their way down his throat.

What you would have seen in his eyes as the giant tumbleweed rolled out on the highway were some of his favorite emotions. Terror and confusion emanated from him as he begged some unknown entity for his life, and then his eyes widened in disbelief just before he bounced off a car and into the grill of a semi-truck.

Five minutes later, Laura and Sarah banged on the door and seconds after that, the deputies and the ambulance pulled in the driveway.

Since the bullet had gone clear through her shoulder, Rhonda would likely be okay. She even fussed at the paramedics as they loaded her into the ambulance.

Laura's face was eerily calm as it drove away. She said to Bash, "I'm coming with you to look for him."

The deputies were wary of that but remembered Don's advice and stood by while she climbed in the truck.

Audi laid her hand on the door and said, "You probably won't find him—at least not much of him."

Laura and Sarah exchanged looks with the deputies. The witches understood, but Bash and Chuck could only imagine what they would find.

The Sheriff's Department closed the interstate for miles while they gathered up pieces of Kyle and threw them in the back of the truck. Laura peered over the side and made a face, then leaned against a sign that read, 'State Prison – Do Not Pick Up Hitchhikers'. From the middle of the road, she heard Chuck on his phone.

"Hey Don, we found your escapee. He's all over the fuckin' highway, man." There was a pause and then he said, "well, do you want these pieces back or not?"

"He was trapped in the tumbleweed, Laura." Bash ran a hand through his hair. "What in the hell did Audi do to him?

Laura thought of Rhonda's small frame bleeding through the bandages and said, "'What didn't she do?' is a better question." She plucked a thorn from his collar, "Do you really want to know?"

We learn in Heaven's Lost that the realtor, Chase Markham, presented Sebastian Scott with two houses when he moved to town. Chase would never admit it, but Bash speculated that one of them was haunted. They should have known that there are lots of reasons for a house to act weird, especially in Chuparosa.

The Saguaro Sylph

Deputy Sheriff Sebastian Scott arched an eyebrow at Billy Tate, exasperated on behalf of his friend and boss, Chuck Ruiz. They'd been listening for thirty minutes as Chuck grew more and more agitated during his phone conversation with the county administration office.

"I ordered horse tack, but you sent me radios," Chuck explained for the fifth time. "Right, but I still need the tack. Okay, I'll hold." Chuck leaned back in his chair and called to them from his office, "Can you believe this shit, Bash?"

Bash could absolutely believe it. In the few years he'd served the tiny town of Chuparosa, Arizona, he'd learned not to be surprised by anything the county did or didn't do.

"No," Chuck said to the new person on the phone, "I just told her that we got radios instead of the tack I ordered...tack is reins and halters and—" he took a moment for quiet astonishment before clarifying, "for the horses, man."

Drew looked up from his book and laughed. "It's gonna take him all day to sort that out."

Andrew Clarke had found himself with some rare time off and made the station first on his list of stops for the day. He'd come to visit his friends but as one of the town's clergymen he found the sheriff's station, or more specifically, the jail, a place where on occasion he could do some good. Unusually for a Saturday there had been no arrests and they'd spent the morning bitching about the heat and making fun of each other.

"What have you got today, Drew? Demonology 101?" Billy teased.

Drew closed his book and held it up so they could see the cover. "The Complete Book of Superstition, Prophecy and Luck."

"Are you fucking kidding me?" Bash reached for it and began to flip through the pages. They gave Drew a lot of shit, but the information contained in his books had many times been instrumental in helping them out of a jam.

Indeed, Drew's next errand was a meeting with Chuparosa's librarian. Hannah Banks had texted him earlier that she'd received a small shipment of territorial history books he might want to read. His interests tended toward the supernatural but, though he didn't share Bash's fascination with the wild west, he was always ready to learn more about his adopted state's early history. He frequently found that the two interests intersected.

Billy turned to Bash. "Make sure you study hard in the section about luck. What are you doing at work anyway? Isn't this your eighth day in a row?"

Bash thumbed in Chuck's direction. "Because Drew's right about that call taking all day and besides, Laura's at NAU this weekend makin' Brian buy new clothes for graduation."

"Heh, heh," Billy chuckled, "the boy will look good whether he wants to or not."

Drew packed up his satchel and when he stood to leave, the others asked him to give Hannah their regards. As the door closed behind him, the phone rang at the front desk and a few seconds after Billy answered, he said, "Slow down, Chase. Where are you?"

He waved for Bash's attention and put the call on speaker mode. The garbled sound couldn't hide that fact that Chase was under significant stress.

"I'm in the...the house." He stuttered. "You know which house." The line went dead before he could continue.

"What do you suppose that was about?" Billy wondered.

Bash rubbed his goatee while he thought about it. "Isn't he still trying to unload that place at the end of Agave Street?"

Chase Markham was the town's only realtor but did most of his business in Phoenix since few people moved in or out of Chuparosa. Still, there were a couple of homes, like the one rotting empty on Agave, that he was determined to find families for. Billy remembered seeing an 'open house' sign for it at Arley's gas station earlier in the week.

"I believe so," He confirmed.

"Alright, I'll go check it out." Bash felt his pockets for his keys and put on his cowboy hat.

"Careful," Billy warned, "Rhonda says that house has a foul energy."

"When did she tell you that?"

"I ran into her at Racine's for coffee on Tuesday."

"You ran into her for coffee?"

"Why don't you mind your own damn business and then mind yourself around that house. It's like I used to tell my boys when they were dating: you don't want to get something on you that you can't wash off."

Bash made a face. "Thanks, Billy."

He whistled for Watson, but the enormous German Shepherd was already pacing by the door. He grabbed the handle and then turned back to see Billy stacking and unstacking the same manila folders, mumbling to himself about nosy deputies and boring Saturdays.

"You wanna take a ride out there with me?" Bash asked.

Billy clasped his hands together. "You mean I can finally be part of the action?" His sarcasm could not belie his genuine excitement as he quickly forwarded the phone and holstered his gun. Billy wasn't a badged officer, but everyone in Chuparosa was armed and Bash would have thought him senile if the old man had left it behind.

"Should I film this ride along with my phone?" Billy asked. "Maybe we could sell the footage to one of those reality television shows. They usually prefer to see the town's finest officers, but I suppose you'll do."

"Are you comin' or not?"

Billy called out to Chuck, "I'm going with Turner and Hooch!"

Chuck waved a dismissive hand and shouted into the phone, "What difference does it make how many radios? I don't need the radios…"

The cloud of dust that kicked up from underneath the run-down county pickup's tires was the only other thing on the road that afternoon and Billy stared through the passenger window with dismay.

"I hate to tell you this, Sheriff, but your reality show sucks."

On Agave Street Bash pulled next to the mailbox at the end of the driveway behind an old Pontiac with the license plate CHAS3M.

"There's his car," he said.

Billy rolled his eyes. "Hey, you're pretty good at this detective thing."

Bash ignored him and headed to the front door with Watson. He tried the handle when there was no answer, but it was locked, which was strange if Chase had been planning to show the house.

There was a heaviness in the air as they circled the property that made him uneasy and when Watson paused to sniff around under the back door window, Bash cupped his hands to his face and peered in the kitchen. He was almost afraid of what he would see but other than an abandoned paper coffee cup on the counter there was no sign of Chase.

Billy started to say something, but bash shushed him. "Do you hear that?"

He listened for a minute and then he too heard a

muffled yelp coming from inside. Bash used a loose brick from the porch to break the glass and reached in to unlock the door. Though there was nothing blocking the entryway, it took the strength of both men to push it open and Billy had to lean against the stove top once they were inside to catch his breath.

"You're not gettin' soft, are you?" Unwilling to admit that he too was winded from the effort, Bash led the way to the living room, hollering, "Chase! Chase are you in here?"

Though the late afternoon sun shone through all the bare windows, the house seemed especially dark and when Bash flipped on the overhead light, nothing happened.

"The power was probably cut a long time ago," Billy offered. "This place has been empty for years."

They searched each room but the only living thing they encountered was a Whiptail lizard. It skittered up Billy's pant leg, motivating the older man to achieve a range of motion that Bash guessed he'd not attempted in decades. Before he had time to comment on the spectacle beyond an indiscreet guffaw, Watson's ears perked up and a moment later they again heard a soft cry from somewhere in the house.

"Let's look again," Bash said, but as they made their way back down the hall, each of the home's faucets came on full stream, sputtering and spraying and drowning out the sound they searched for.

"Dammit." Billy twisted the knobs over the hallway bathroom sink every which way with no success. The plugs were stuck too and soon the water flowed over the bowl and flooded the tile.

Bash had a similar experience in the kitchen,

eventually giving up after the rusted shutoff valve crumbled in his hands. Sloshing back through the living room, he stopped in front of a wardrobe closet he hadn't noticed before and began to shiver as ice crystals formed on his wet clothes.

"What the hell?" As he reached out for the wooden doors there was a knock from the inside. Watson barked a warning, but Bash waved him off. "Chase?" He called out and jerked open the double doors, which wrenched themselves out of his grasp and slammed shut.

"Bash!" He and Watson followed the sound of Billy's voice to the main bedroom where Chase Markham lay tied to the four-poster bed by the strands of an unraveled, braided wool rug.

Though he was fully clothed, Billy covered his eyes and hollered, "What kind of freaky shit are you into Chase?"

Bash was more troubled by the fact that Chase hadn't been there when they searched the room before.

"Cut me loose!"

"What's her name?" Bash tried unsuccessfully to suppress his laughter as he unclipped the knife from his belt. His smile faded though when he noticed that Chase's hands were purple from lack of circulation and that his wrists were bloody. Either Chase had a lover with some pretty intense appetites, or he and Billy had surprised someone in the middle of a violent crime.

Chase squirmed while Bash sawed at the ropes, making the task nearly impossible, and then bounded off the bed when he was finally freed. Bash had hoped Chase would confess to an extramarital affair, but as he feared that wasn't the case.

"I wasn't with anyone," Chase insisted, clenching

his fists over and over to get the feeling back in his hands. "It's this house." He stumbled around the room. "This house hates people."

Bash thought of his unsettling experience at the wardrobe and rubbed the bridge of his nose. "You tried to sell me this house, asshole."

"Back then I thought you could handle it, but no one can. We have to get out of here."

They slogged over the wet carpet to the front door which Bash discovered would not open. He pulled and pulled and then Chase pulled with him, but it wouldn't budge.

"Why are you wet?"

"In case you didn't you notice, everything is wet." Billy groused. "By the way, the kitchen door won't open either."

"This is not good." Chase began to hyperventilate and leaned against the wardrobe to steady himself.

"Stay away from that closet," Bash cautioned, "it's a bad place."

"That's called an armoire," Billy corrected.

"Arm war?"

"Armoire. It's French, you idiot."

"French for what?"

"Closet."

"Billy, I swear to god—"

"You might want to pray to god instead." Billy stared out the window. "'Cause it's getting dark, and that armoire is the least of our worries."

He had never been so wrong.

Again, they heard the muffled cry they'd originally

mistaken for Chase. The three men gaped at the armoire where it appeared to be coming from and then realized it was more of a song than a sob. Bash whistled a bit of "Don't You Forget About Me" and took a startled step sideways when whatever it was whistled the tune back at him.

Chase leaned in close. "What's going on in there?"

Then the doors flew open, and he let out a howl as an unseen force pulled him inside. Bash lurched toward him and grabbed for the doors, but they slammed shut on his fingers so hard that the skin scraped clean off his knuckles as he pulled them free.

"God dammit Bash, hold tight 'till I get back." Billy ran for the bathroom but returned empty handed a few minutes later. "There's not even a nasty old Band-Aid stuck to the shelf in there." He complained.

Bash dismissed his concern. "We've got bigger problems." The wardrobe doors creaked open slowly to reveal that the entire thing was empty.

"So, the closet ate Chase," Billy grumbled. "You got an axe in your truck?"

"Yeah but..." Bash tugged on the front door handle again to remind him that they couldn't go outside. "Anyway, we'll never get Chase back if we chop that thing up."

While Billy mulled over the pros and cons of that particular state of affairs, Bash brought a chair from the kitchen. "I have an idea."

He threw the chair against the picture window, but it bounced off the glass and flew into bits against the wall across the room.

"Well, shit." He stared at the shards for a while and then said, "Okay, I have another idea."

"Are you still with Hannah Banks?"

Drew recognized the tone of Bash's voice when he answered the phone and didn't bother to ask him why he wanted to know. He switched to speaker mode and said, "She's right here."

"Hannah, what do you know about the empty house on Agave Street?"

"Let's see..." She twisted her mouth as she thought about it. "There have been a few houses on that property, but the others burned down over the years. The one that stands now was built in the late nineteen eighties. Everyone assumes it's haunted, but no one really knows why."

"Oh, it's haunted alright," Bash confirmed.

"What are you doing there?"

"That's a long story, but we have upset this house in a big way. It took Chase Markham and now it won't let us out."

"Sheriff Scott, you of all people know better than to—"

"Dammit woman, we didn't do it on purpose."

"Well, something's trying to get your attention."

"It absolutely has my attention." He pressed his shirt tail against his fingers in an attempt stop the bleeding. "I just don't know what it wants."

"Have you got salt with you?" Drew asked.

"Of course I do."

"Put yourselves in a circle and stay there," he said. "I'm on my way."

"Even though the Saguaros were moved, that house has so much character," Hannah sighed, "it was such a shame because they grew the most beautiful blooms every year."

"What Saguaros?"

"There were two," she explained. "The original builders designed the entire property around them, but Chase had them relocated this year. He said they were too dramatic—too much trouble, but they must have been there for at least a hundred years."

"Hmmm." Drew gathered up his books and kissed her cheek. "Thank you, Hannah. Librarians are the angels of information."

"You would know." She smiled. "Just be careful."

"Here." Bash dug a small pouch from his front shirt pocket and tossed it to Billy. "Make a circle."

He moved to an area of the entryway in the living room where the water hadn't reached and began to empty the pouch while Bash tried again to get the attention of whatever had whistled to him before from the armoire.

He was rewarded almost instantly with a response, but also with a stiff breeze that froze the water in the carpet and blew the salt off the tile, melding it with the ice crystals.

Billy put his hands on his hips. "That's not supposed to happen, is it?"

"I don't know." Bash said. "I'm not a witch."

"You sleep with one," Billy snapped. "Haven't you learned anything at all?"

Their argument was cut short when they noticed a shadow crossing in front of the window, pausing and then traveling to the back of the house. Watson sprinted to the kitchen door as it opened and a second later their senses were jolted back to normal when the rushing of the sink water ceased.

Bash and Billy exchanged looks as Drew followed Watson to the living room. Bash hollered, "Wait!", but the warning came just as Drew slid across the frozen carpet, flailing wildly in a skid that took him all the way to the tile by the door.

"Jesus Christ!" Drew panted.

"How did you get the water turned off?" Bash asked as he steadied him.

"That's your question?" Drew could only imagine the aches and pains he would wake up with after those acrobatics, assuming he survived to wake up at all. "It shut off by itself when I walked in."

Satisfied that he wouldn't be soaked by the faucets anymore, Watson shook his entire body and sprayed them with icy water.

Bash frowned. "Thanks buddy."

"Hannah was right when she said this house wants your attention." Drew looked around and shivered, as much from the cold as the grim atmosphere. "I have a theory, but I need you to tell me everything."

He listened intently as Bash relayed the day's events and as Billy added editorial commentary.

"I don't think you guys upset this house," Drew said finally. "Something else is here."

Just then every cabinet door, closet door and the doors to every room began to open and slam shut over and over. Watson growled and the men put their hands over their ears while the deafening clatter went on and on until Drew shouted, "Okay, Okay! I understand!"

"I guess you're right," Bash said lowering his hands. "What is it then?"

"Sometimes, powerful connections are formed in

nature, particularly in a place like Chuparosa that vibrates with otherworldly energy, and there are creatures who protect and thrive off of those unions. Chase relocated the two Saguaros that used to be in front of this house, but they were ancient and most likely interdependent with the land we're standing on. The sylph that lived among them was probably frightened by the noise and the workmen and ran to hide—"

"In the house." Bash finished his sentence.

"What the hell is a sylph?" Billy asked.

"An air spirit," Drew explained. "They don't have a body like ours but they're strong."

Bash looked down at his shredded knuckles. "They sure are."

"This house or this land *is* haunted by something—you said Chase told you it was worse than ever—and I bet it's annoyed by the presence of the sylph and wants the intruder out."

Every light in every room blinked on and off in agreement with Drew. He turned in a circle scanning for details. "She doesn't have a body, but she could appear somehow if she wanted to."

"Why in the world would she want to?" Billy groused. "She probably lived happily for decades with those cacti until that dipshit decided to play gardener."

"She did though." Bash whistled another bit of the eighties tune and after a second the sylph whistled it back to him.

"See? But I don't get it." He spoke slowly in an attempt to keep his teeth from chattering. "The desert is lousy with cactus, and she could go anywhere."

Drew shook his head. "She's trapped here, or at

least she thinks she is."

"Here's your chance, Bash. You know how you love to rescue damsels in distress."

Bash bristled at Billy's joke but only because it was true. His need to protect others, particularly women, ran deep and he would be lying if he said the predicament of the sylph hadn't already melted his heart.

He approached the armoire and said, "Give us back back our, um, friend, and I'll take you to another Saguaro. It's not far. I promise."

To the others he added, "Hopefully it's not already occupied."

"Don't go borrowin' trouble," Billy mumbled.

There was a crashing noise inside the armoire, and they hopped back as the doors burst open and Chase tumbled out. He was followed by a being just under a foot tall that they could only make out due to the dust particles that clung to her wispy frame. She whistled in alarm as Watson gave her a sniff, but Bash said, "Easy boy", and the former hellhound bowed his head, allowing her to skirt around him.

The front door flung itself open and Bash felt himself being pushed from behind. He gave the others a nervous glance over his shoulder and then slowly escorted the sylph outside to where the asphalt ended and the desert took over.

"I'll bet it feels good to get some fresh air," he told her.

She whistled an unfamiliar little tune in response.

There was a ring of Saguaros at the end of the street that he and Laura had once thought was a portal to the Other Side but if it was, they couldn't open it. Perhaps the sylph would have better luck.

It was difficult to see the sylph in general but in the dark she was invisible except for the little noise she made as she whizzed around.

"My girlfriend loves this place," Bash said. "Do you think you could be happy here?"

There was no answer, but a soft warm breeze brushed across his body. After a moment, the air around him stilled as she presumably set about moving into her new home. He smiled to himself as he walked back to the house, whistling their song.

He found Billy in the front yard castigating Chase for not leaving things well enough alone. "You're from Chuparosa for god's sake, you ought to know better."

An obnoxious rumble came from the other end of the street as Chuck pulled up in his barely running truck.

"How did you know we were here?" Bash asked.

"Hannah Banks called to check on you guys." He eyed their wet clothes and Chase Markham's wild-eyed expression. "Is everything okay, man?"

"It is now," Bash said. "Is everything sorted out with the county?"

"I got an email from a supervisor before I left." Chuck smacked his hand against his forehead and said, "He's very sorry about the mix-up and they're sending us another dozen radios."

While not necessarily the supernatural kind, there is an awful lot of magic simmering under the surface of self-contained female rage.

Calls for a Silver Alert

Drew's head snapped up as the door slammed shut behind Monica. Her shoulders shot to her ears and she squeezed her eyes closed as if doing so would make her invisible to everyone who turned to stare.

"Welcome in." Drew's smile was warm as he motioned to an empty seat in the circle.

Alcoholism ran rampant in Chuparosa, but the bottle tended to be the least dangerous of their local demons. Pastor Andrew Clarke was well aware of what haunted his congregation and how loathe they were to offer themselves up to town gossip. Still, he dutifully scheduled Monday night Alcoholics Anonymous and Tuesday afternoon Al-Anon meetings that were open to anyone brave enough, or desperate enough to trust their neighbors with a peek into their lives.

On that particular Tuesday, Monica's attendance

brought the number to four, if you counted Stacy Wilson's fussy toddler. Drew heaved an internal sigh on her behalf because Monica and her husband, Jim, had lived in town as long as he could remember. Recent empty nesters, they traveled a lot and volunteered around town and, as was usually the case, gave no indication that anything was less than perfect at home.

"I'm sorry," Monica stammered, "late as usual." She issued more half audible apologies as the group scooted their chairs around to accommodate her.

She was late because Jim had left late for his class. In fact, *she* was never late for anything, but her husband frequently stalled as they were leaving the house, pre-gaming their outings with a couple of beers or a shot of something so he could stand the socializing he said she forced him into. You would never know he hated it so much though, as outgoing as he was.

Drew opened the floor to Stacy, their inaugural member, who briefly recounted her story for the group. She felt safe speaking freely at such meetings because everyone in town already knew what she would say. Her father had nearly beaten her to death during a haboob the previous summer and afterward, he'd fired on Sheriff Scott, who shot him in the chest and ended that family's lifelong struggle with addiction right then and there.

Careful not to look directly at Monica, Drew asked if anyone else would like to share. Sixteen-year-old Ryan attended on orders from his social worker for a fumbled attempt at suicide after his girlfriend died from a methamphetamine overdose.

He kicked at a chip in the linoleum and grumbled, "You know what happened."

Drew had intended to steer the conversation toward the idea of acceptance, but instead decided to address the courage it took for all of them to be there.

Monica shifted in her seat feeling ridiculous, not courageous. She had nothing like their problems. She hadn't lost anyone and she wasn't abused, not really. If anything, she was spoiled. He could be mean, but Jim never laid a hand on her, and he lavished her with gifts. She reminded herself that he really wasn't even mean if you compared him to Stacy's father. *Good god, that man was a monster.*

She kept her head bowed. "Is it alright if I don't have anything to say?"

"Of course."

When the hour was up, Ryan made a bee line to the snack table in the back of the room. Drew brought Rice Krispie treats covered with chocolate chips and had told the boy he could take home the leftovers.

Drew placed a marshmallow square in a napkin and hurried to catch Monica. "Do you have time to stay for a snack?" He held it out to her. "I made these myself."

"I couldn't." Her eyes reddened suddenly, and she looked to the ceiling to keep the tears from falling. "It's not that bad, you know. I'm being silly. It's probably just hormonal."

"*Just* hormonal?" His girlfriend, Sarah Deane, was in perimenopause and there was no *just* about it. In any case, he knew better. "Whatever brought you here today is not silly, and you are always welcome."

"I won't tell, if that's what you're worried about." Stacy offered, hoisting her now screaming toddler to her hip. "I obviously have plenty of other things to do."

Ryan chomped on his second Rice Krispie treat,

mumbling, "Even if I did tell, no one listens to me."

She glanced at the time on her phone and excused herself. Though it was a steamy July day of at least 110°, she was glad that she'd walked to the meeting. Jim would be home, and it was after three so he would be drunk.

Well so what if he is? She asked herself. *You're not his mother. So what if he likes to drink?*

Monica had taken to having their arguments with herself when the last time she brought it up, he said, "You're going to make me an alcoholic if you don't get off my back."

Faced with that responsibility she hadn't mentioned it since and, given her experience at the meeting, Jim was right, she didn't know from alcohol abuse. Even so, she slowed her pace, reluctant to begin their evening. She wouldn't get to spend quality time with her husband; she would have to manage herself around him until he passed out.

Management began as soon as she opened the door. He was sitting at the kitchen table watching a video of himself on his laptop.

She winced as he said, "Look at this! I'm ready to solo on Saturday!"

He was unaware that he was shouting which meant that he'd felt the need to celebrate with gusto after class. Flying lessons at the Glendale airport filled up most of his days since he'd retired from the financial firm he'd devoted much of his life to.

"We'll have to cancel our museum date." She frowned. It wasn't that big of a deal to cancel, but he could have scheduled the class for Friday or Sunday.

"Museum date?"

"The Heard Museum, Jim. With your sister and her husband. We planned this weeks ago."

"You never told me we were going to the museum." He patted her hand. "Honey, you can't expect me to make arrangements around things I didn't know about."

She could swear she told him. They'd discussed it over dinner and then she bought the tickets online. She decided not to argue and took a chance on real communication by asking another question instead.

"What's it like up there?" She'd been in dozens of planes, but Jim was learning to fly a Cesna 172. It was very different from a commercial aircraft and Monica was terrified to go up in something so small. Even so, she hoped he would ease her mind and maybe even take her with him someday.

He either didn't hear her or was ignoring her in favor of his internet search. "This one's a beauty."

"In that case, can I finally tell people about your accomplishment?"

"Absolutely not until I have my license in hand!"

"Alright, alright." To mention his decibel level would be taken as further raining on his parade. Not being in that business anymore, she plucked her library book off the counter, plugged in her earphones, and selected some coffee shop jazz. As predicted, he was out cold on the couch an hour later, leaving her free to enjoy their big bed by herself.

One of Monica's favorite things was getting him up early after a night like that. Since he always swore he was never *that* drunk, he couldn't ever admit to being hungover, and the next morning she took perverse pleasure in his misery as they stood in line for a table at Racine's Diner.

She waved to Molly, who glared in their direction before ducking behind the counter.

"Did you see the way Molly looked at us? That was strange. I wonder if she's okay."

"You probably upset her."

"What? Do you think so? I just saw her the other day."

"You know how you are sometimes. Look, we're never going to get a table here. I'll take you to the city. I want to look at some golf clubs anyway."

All morning Monica wondered what she could possibly have done to upset Molly. They weren't close, but she considered them to be friends. Her anxiety was at its peak when Jim dropped her at home and headed for the driving range to try out his new gear.

"Don't worry so much," he said as he left, "I'm sure she'll get over it, whatever you did."

Molly would be working in her restaurant all day, so Monica couldn't call her to discuss it. She decided to follow up on something else that had been eating at her and opened her laptop. She searched through her deleted emails, cursing Outlook and its inability to understand the simplest of keywords, until eventually finding what she had absolutely known was there. The email she'd sent Jim with the receipt for the Heard Museum tickets, to which he'd responded, "Oh yay, another museum," followed by the barfing smiley emoji.

She sat back in her chair and stared at the screen, so lost in thought that she jumped when the pop-ding of the Facebook Messenger app sent a notification to Jim's laptop, still open on the table. The message was from

Molly.

Without hesitating, she opened it up and read: `For the last time, leave me alone.`

She scrolled through the message thread to learn that Jim had been hitting on Molly since her husband passed away three years earlier. Apparently, he'd done it in person until he discovered the social media app, from which Molly was threatening to block him.

Monica opened his email and at the very top was a message from Kristi, the flight school receptionist, announcing her intent to tell her boss if Jim didn't leave her alone.

"These women are much smarter than me," she said to the air.

There was no password on his laptop and no secret email accounts. His actions were so brazen, so obvious, that she was in shock. But why hide anything if he knew he could convince her that it was all her own fault. Monica knew exactly how it would go. He would say she was unsupportive, a constant nag, and that her hormones were making her too crazy to live with. He would tell everyone that he loved her more than anything, but that she drove him away.

The fact that she could predict his defense made her sick to her stomach, but it also gave her an idea. With freedom she hadn't known she wanted until that moment dangling within reach, Monica began making calls.

On Saturday morning, Jim whistled to himself as he got ready for his solo flight. From bed, Monica watched him take a few swigs of the bourbon he hid in the Listerine bottle and then brush his teeth.

She rose and stood next to him, peering into the mirror. She didn't look at him as she brushed her hair and asked, "Can we talk about Molly and Kristi?"

He was stunned by her accusation and shoved her against the shower door, incensed by how she'd taken control of the situation before he even knew there was a situation. He regained his composure as quickly as he'd lost it and released her with a casual chuckle. He was cornered, but he was good.

"You sound even crazier than usual, honey. Don't you think it's time to get some help? Next week, we'll make an appointment for another hormone check." He kissed her on the forehead, feigning concern. "They have better treatment now, and you don't have to suffer like this."

The door had barely closed behind him when Monica made another call.

Deputy Sheriffs Chuck Ruiz and Sebastian Scott were headed back to Chuparosa after a meeting with their Executive Command downtown.

"Look, all I'm sayin'," Bash complained, "is that these mandatory Saturday meetings are bullshit."

"You're not wrong, man, but you can't tell him to go——"

Just then Billy Tate's irritated voice crackled over the radio from dispatch. "Did you two see that new silver alert on the 101?"

"Yeah," they answered in unison, having just passed the ADOT marquee advising them to be on the lookout for a gray Cadillac Escalade.

"Well guess what? Monica Lewis called it in on Jim."

"No kiddin'?" Chuck hadn't heard anything about

Jim's health declining, but he *was* roughly a decade older than Monica.

"This is Jim, the finance guy we're talkin' about, right?" Bash couldn't believe it either.

"Same one," Billy confirmed. "She says he went nuts and tried to put her through a wall this morning. Then he left the house talking about he's a pilot or something. He's on his way to the Glendale Airport and she's afraid he's gonna try to steal a plane."

They arrived at the airport to find Jim arguing with a pilot instructor, who clearly didn't know who he was. That's because days earlier, Monica had called Kristi to cancel his class. The instructor in front of him was not his and had never seen him before.

"Jim?" Chuck called out, "What's goin' on, man?"

"What are you doing here, Sheriff? Are they making you fly the helicopters yourself now?"

"Is there a problem?" Bash asked the instructor.

"I never told anyone," Jim interrupted, "but I'm supposed to take my first solo flight today. Nobody here seems to know anything about it."

The instructor shrugged and shook his head, and Bash motioned for him to move a safe distance away from them. In his excitement, Jim had taken one too many shots that morning, and his speech was a little slurred. He was used to being in control of every situation and his eyes went wild with anger after being defied twice in one day.

"Let's go in and talk about it," Chuck suggested.

It was hot on the tarmac and Jim felt he could definitely use a drink of water, so he followed them to the office.

Inside, Kristi flashed a brilliant smile from behind

the desk and when Bash asked her if Jim had a lesson that day, she let the smile fade to a look of confusion and said, "No sir. No Jim on the schedule today."

"Kristi, you know I was supposed to solo today."

Chuck held an arm out to stop Jim from leaning over the desk. "That's close enough."

Jim walked to the window and looked maniacally from the plane outside, to Kristi, to the deputies and back. He had no idea what was happening, and he could not handle it. He lunged for Kristi, but Chuck and Bash were ready for that, and they slammed his face against the desk, cuffing his hands behind him and setting him down hard on the floor to wait for the paramedics.

"This is ridiculous," Jim slurred and toppled over.

Once they rode away in the ambulance, Kristi picked up the phone, and Monica paced the house for a while after they spoke. Her newfound courage was overwhelming, but there was no turning back.

The last call she made that day was to a divorce attorney in Phoenix. There could be consequences but thanks to Jim, she had learned a whole new skillset that she would fully employ to make sure that he was the only one who paid for her actions.

I have no excuse for this one and I won't hold my breath for a call from the folks that make Hallmark movies; but maybe you'll enjoy an 'enemies to lovers' type romance that includes a bitter divorce, an angry poltergeist, and a couple of nosy bobcats.

Desert Falls

Interstate 10 *Just East of Blythe, California 1988*
The August sun seared ugly red splotches into the delicate skin on Penny's forehead, but she wouldn't stop to raise the cover on her convertible Volkswagen. In fact, she undid the banana clip that restrained her hair and pressed her foot all the way down on the accelerator of her *getaway* car.

The record company insisted to Claudia, Penny's doubtful manager, that it would be public relations gold if Penny Poole were to be photographed in that car on Sunset Strip. They'd included a not-so-subtle hint for her to get one of the Coreys in the passenger seat too. That Penny had only driven a few times seemed to matter little. Perhaps that was why it never occurred to them that she would use their extravagant birthday gift to run as far away as possible.

She caught a glimpse of herself in the review mirror, sunburned with chapped lips and matted hair blowing in the wind. Claudia would have had a stroke at the sight of her. Penny wondered how much it would cost to fix her appearance and how long her parents would hold it over her head after the amount was deducted from her royalties.

The petite pop star had burst onto the scene with a single hit song written for the boy she loved. The boy they took her away from who was even then off to college without her. Penny's father had recorded her singing and submitted the tape to a low-level music industry friend of his. It was less of an overnight success story for her than it was for her father's friend, who seemed to make more money than anyone off of her sweet little love song.

Her plans were to study journalism and travel the world covering protests and hijackings for Sixty Minutes. Instead, with dollar signs in their eyes, her parents had signed a contract that essentially handed their young daughter over to Claudia and her corral of pretty, talented hopefuls. A grueling year later she was poised to release a full album, which did not include any of the other songs she'd written. Her lack of input on the record bothered her less than Claudia's subsequent announcement that she was to take acting lessons in preparation for a role in a new sitcom.

After stealing Claudia's credit card, Penny bought a tourist map of the Southwest and figured she could make it all the way to Arizona before anyone noticed she was gone. She'd picked out a golf resort outside of

Phoenix called The Wigwam and would contact her parents from there, threatening them that she would never come home if they didn't let her use her money for college instead of acting lessons.

It took a while for her heart rate to slow after the frantic business of getting on the freeway. Traffic was awful, even in the predawn before rush hour but the slow pace allowed her to stay in her lane and get used to the road habits of the other drivers.

It was an easy straight line to Arizona, and after managing a stop for gas in Tonopah, her confidence soared. The attendant told her that The Wigwam was only about an hour away. Though he was clearly suspicious of the circumstances that would lead a wild looking teenager through the desert in a fabulous car, he decided in the end that it was none of his business, gave her some water, and left her alone.

His guilt would haunt him until the end of his days after the highway patrol showed up to question him about the dead girl they'd found in a Cabriolet that rolled into a ravine just outside of Chuparosa.

The attendant's inaction was only one of the forces conspiring against Penny on that day. The factory fault in one of her front tires couldn't contend with the heat softened asphalt on a remote highway overpass that had been long ignored by the Department of Transportation. For a split second after the tire blew, she thought the resounding bang was the bridge collapsing but then realized with a shock that her precious getaway car was rolling end over end off the side.

Even after standing for hours over her broken body, she could not piece together the last moments of the crash. It must have been horrific, but she would have relished every broken bone if it meant that the mourning in her soul would cease.

She cried endless, tearless sobs until out of nowhere that night, two bobcats approached and dropped wildflowers around the vehicle. They offered some to her in what she could only imagine were their condolences. They remained until the grim site was discovered days later and watched with her as the car was towed out of the ravine and her body driven away in a quiet ambulance.

The desert was lonely and every now and then she would call to them. The bobcats brought her more flowers and her grief lessened for a while when they played under the bridge. Soon their games could not compete with her growing sorrow and, ravenous for warmer feelings, she took to the road searching for anything to feed her spirit.

At first, she found only the despair that surrounded other car accidents, but then came upon a man with a flat tire. He was furious, spitting at the ground and kicking the spare and Penny was thrilled. Why had she not thought of it before?

As the years went by, she learned that rage would cover up her sadness better than anything. It also spilled over into the spaces around her, killing the flowers and running off her bobcat friends. It even wafted into the cars driving by, starting senseless arguments among the passengers. Nothing kept her pain from returning though, and after a while Penny grew desperate. What was left of her sanity eventually dissolved and she stalked the desert screaming her hit song on an endless loop, drowning out the loudest of the howling coyotes.

She stalked and screamed until one day a housing development broke ground across the highway. Shortly afterward, the hapless site supervisor named Luke Shepherd moved with his wife into the first model home.

They were an unhappy, mismatched couple whose angry fights fed Penny's bitter soul to bursting. It was when they finally divorced, and sadness settled over the lonely house that Penny remembered her own dreadful loss and began to take revenge on Luke.

"Desert Falls?" The hardware store's cashier studied Luke's purchase order and shook his head. "What falls?"

"There's a waterfall in the mountains," Luke said glaring down at a text from his ex-wife.

"That miserable trickle?"

The cashier laughed so sharply that Luke's head snapped up. "All the tourists take that trail," he argued, though he'd never taken it himself.

"Tourists." The cashier sniffed. "That's everything you need to know about the waterfall."

The housing development known as Desert Falls was only one of a handful of problems that Luke supervised at the time. The construction site was plagued with disasters and delays, surprising no one in a town known for its oddities. Chuparosa hosted any number supernatural occurrences and though not many people talked about it, everyone seemed to know everything about them.

Luke had gotten used to it, even coming to an unspoken agreement with the three-foot-tall jackrabbit that routinely chewed through the cable television wires on the outside of his house. After some experimentation, he'd solved the problem with a combination of greens and sliced bell peppers set out during every full moon. Not just any greens, mind you. It had to be escarole.

Once, when the grocery store was out of it, he tried to sweeten the offering with strawberries instead, but that misstep resulted in a loss of signal on Super Bowl Sunday. He was able to migrate his friends to Isaac's Oasis for the game, but they would never let him forget that he somehow managed to offend a rabbit with a salad.

He left the grumpy cashier and shifted the box of supplies on his hip to read another text from Trudy. He'd been ignoring her repeated requests to forward the Christmas decorations and she was furious, announcing that she would be there to pick them up on Saturday.

"Fine," he said it out loud but decided not to type out a response.

He didn't miss her anymore, but for some reason he'd been reluctant to release their last connection. In truth, those stupid plastic ornaments meant nothing to either of them since, because of his job, they'd only spent one Christmas together—their last.

The box had become a prop she often pulled out to show what he'd missed out on, but by the time their divorce was final he viewed it as yet another symbol of what they'd lost, and he couldn't believe she wanted to take it with her.

Early in their marriage he was consumed with guilt and he hated being away from her but he truly believed he was building them a better life. She was gone by the time he was finally able to take time off and he resented her lack of faith in him.

Next door to the hardware store, Hannah Banks shooed out the last of the library patrons. She gathered her books, lunch bag, water bottle and coffee thermos before remembering that her keys were still at the bottom of her purse. Bouts of forgetfulness were the latest annoyances in her journey through perimenopause, but she would not let her hormones bully her into putting all of that stuff down again.

While balancing everything against the door frame, she cursed her cute new purse with its complicated hook and eye closure and then cursed the recent online shopping spree in which it found itself in her Amazon cart.

Headed home at last, she took an extra-long pause before turning onto Main Street. One could hardly say that Chuparosa had anything like a rush hour, but kids were running around at that time of day and big tractors always seemed to come out of nowhere. She proceeded with what was probably a little more caution than necessary until the guy in the giant Silverado behind her laid on his horn with impatience.

Hannah was not in the mood to be bullied by him either and threw open the door of her little Ford Ranger to confront him.

"Hey!" She marched over to his door. "Where's the fire, asshole?"

Holy crap. He knew he'd made a dick move, but Luke hadn't expected her to be so mad. He didn't open his door or roll down his window, but the pretty brunette staring up at him with her hands on her hips was unmoved. He motioned for her to get back into her truck, but she stood there a minute more, then flipped him off and turned on her heel.

He did get out of his truck then, irrationally offended by her gesture and calling after her as he followed. "You don't have to be so obnoxious!" When she stopped in her tracks, he suddenly regretted every life choice he'd made that afternoon.

"You're calling *me* obnoxious?" Hannah whirled on him but hadn't realized he was so close behind her and bounced her nose off his chest. "Ow." She staggered back and glared at him.

He lowered his head and stepped in front of her pickup so she couldn't see him laugh. Her eyes widened when he did, and she snapped at him, "Get back!"

Is she seriously worried about me touching her puny little truck? Before he could argue, she jerked on his arm to pull him away from the street.

"Jesus, lady!"

She knocked them both off balance sending him and his Diamondbacks cap in different directions before falling with him to the asphalt. His fury dissolved as he rolled away from her and a crop tractor loaded down with hay rumbled past, only just missing him. Luke sighed with relief and looked up to see her standing over him with a shaky hand held out.

"That guy wasn't paying attention at all," he griped as she hauled him to his feet.

"Oh great," she muttered as Sheriff Chuck Ruiz pulled over next to them.

"Everything okay here?" Chuck looked her up and down. Her eyes were red, and blood seeped from her knee through a fresh tear in her jeans. "Hannah?"

"It's alright, Sheriff." The people who had been watching them through the windows were now coming out of the shops to stare and Hannah frowned, knowing she'd be the star of the town gossip for the rest of the week.

"We were talking, and that damn tractor almost hit us."

"Yeah." Chuck shook his head. "I've warned the farmers not to come this way but it's the quickest route through town."

She limped toward her pickup. "Can I go?"

"Do you want me to take a look at that knee?"

"No, I'm fine." The episode had her shaken and she wanted to get going before the men saw her cry.

Chuck wasn't convinced that she'd told him the whole story, but he opened the door for her. They watched her drive away and then he leveled his gaze on Luke. "Do you have anything to add to her story?"

The Sheriff had a reputation for being an affable badass, known to have gone head-to-head with any number of Chuparosa's inhuman elements.

Hannah had given Luke an out, but not wanting to become one of Chuck's human targets, he confessed, "We were having a stupid argument when the tractor came by." He rubbed the bridge of his nose while mentally processing the incident. "She probably saved my life, or at least saved me from a trip to the hospital."

"So, you're not mad at her anymore?"

"I wasn't really mad at her." Luke plucked his baseball cap off the ground and slapped it against his thigh before putting it back on. "You ever have one of those days when you should have just stayed in bed?"

Chuck laughed. "You have no idea, man."

Luke made dinner with some trepidation that night, looking over his shoulder as he fried up a hamburger patty. He and Trudy had always felt an extra presence in the house, one that made them a little nervous. It was usually just a creepy sensation or a sound they couldn't place, though sometimes they distinctly heard someone humming a song.

Occasionally dishes would fall out of the cabinets, and they once found all their shoelaces tied together in the closet. After Trudy moved away, whatever it was became more brazen with its attacks. Luke assumed it was trying to get rid of him too, but he was a stubborn man with no intention of giving up his dream house.

Even so, he was careful to keep his fingers away from the blade while slicing a tomato. With one near miss already under his belt that day he wasn't taking any chances with a poltergeist lurking around.

A pang of loneliness shot through him as his thoughts centered on Hannah and the sexy way her eyes narrowed when she glared at him. He wondered how badly her knee was hurt and if he should check in. It wouldn't take too many calls around town to get her number, but he'd been lucky she didn't accuse him of road rage earlier and decided not to press his luck by stalking her.

Even with his favorite mustard, the burger and tomato weren't that exciting, so he rooted around in the pantry until he found a half-full bag of stale Doritos and took the chips with his plate to the couch. Relieved that there was a cable signal, he flipped to the baseball playoffs, hoping to distract himself. The last thing he needed was a pain in the ass librarian bitching at him all the time, no matter how he'd felt when he took her hand.

Penny had been excited when Luke came home slamming the door and she circled the couch in a frantic whir, hoping that he was angry. It was a fix she needed so badly that her spirit vibrated with anticipation. His confusion and yearning were intolerable emotions and she lashed out by flipping his empty plate off the coffee table.

His body stiffened as it shattered on the tile. "There you are," he mumbled, craning his neck in vain to see her. No ghost appeared to him but there was a wretched feeling in the air that soured the dinner in his stomach.

She flung the remote control at him, but he snatched it out of the air, shouting, "I don't need this tonight!"

She drank in his irritation, only it was over as quickly as it started and replaced with something she hadn't been exposed to in a long time. Hovering over his bed later as he tossed and turned, Penny decided that in lieu of anger, his fear would have to do.

The next day he met Andrew Clarke at Racine's Diner for coffee before they headed to the job site.

Drew had the unusual distinction of being an electrician who moonlighted as a preacher. He led a sort of rag tag congregation called the New Sanctuary and they held services at the YMCA. Since there was no money in God's work, Drew couldn't quit his day job, so Luke frequently took advantage of his electrical expertise.

"Do you see this shit?" He waved his hand at the

downed poles that had held up his temporary power lines the day before. "It's like there was an earthquake in this very spot last night." He swore again as coffee sloshed over his wrist.

Drew couldn't help but laugh. "Chuparosa doesn't adapt very well to change, my friend."

"Are you saying the town itself knocked down those poles?"

Drew raised his eyebrows but didn't answer him, and for that Luke was glad. It was too early in the morning for an existential crisis, so he changed the subject.

"Hey, have you been to the waterfall?"

Drew checked himself before he answered. He'd seen some impressive waterfalls in Chuparosa but never on their Side of the veil. Assuming Luke was referring to the tourist trap, he said, "It's a popular trail but in the end I'm afraid it's not much to look at."

Luke tossed his coffee cup in a trash bin and gazed at the view behind them. "Can you believe I've lived here for five years, and I've never hiked in those mountains."

"It's not the best idea to go out there alone."

"Are you trying to remind me that I'm getting old?"

Drew grimaced. "I'm saying that I hike out there all the time, so give me a call if you'd like a partner. The best trails around here are the unmarked ones that the tourists know nothing about."

What he said was true, but he also didn't want Luke accidentally slipping over to the Other Side with no experience.

Luke nodded absently and changed the subject again. "Does, uh, Hannah Banks go to your church?"

Though it was all over town, Drew didn't let on that he'd heard about their confrontation in the parking lot and how everyone said she'd thrown him in front of a tractor. "On occasion, why?"

"Is she always so—"

"Smart? Thoughtful? Determined?"

With his head down, Luke kicked at the dirt. "I have to admit that I was going to use other words."

"I had a feeling."

"What else do you know about her?"

"She's a widow—he had a heart attack a few years ago."

Luke's expression sobered. He and Trudy weren't likely to ever be friends again, but he couldn't imagine such a thing.

"She has a daughter in Tucson at the University of Arizona," Drew continued. "The girl is something of a hothead, always giving Hannah fits."

"The apple didn't fall too far from that tree," Luke laughed.

"And she's a good friend who has helped me with hours of research."

"You have a pretty high opinion of her."

"I do." Drew grinned and decided to let him in on the rumor mill. "Even if she did try to kill you yesterday."

"What?!"

Having accomplished next to nothing at the job site, Luke went to the library. Darting through the stacks while Hannah eyed him suspiciously from the front desk, he quickly found the right section. Chuparosa being what it was, the library had no shortage of books on paranormal activity and he was hoping to get some help for his problem at home.

Though she thought he was ignoring her, it was in fact taking most of his concentration to read instead of stare. Somehow, Hannah was even more stunning than he remembered from the parking lot. She was in her element while helping out the other patrons, and knowledgeable about the most random of topics. After catching himself more than once letting the words blur on the page while listening to her soothing voice, he decided to get a library card and check the books out to read later.

"Did you do something different with your hair?" he asked, approaching the desk.

She pushed a few strands behind her ear. "I always go a little darker in the fall."

"Probably would have been easier just to get a pumpkin spice latte and call it good." He bit his tongue in self-punishment as his awkward joke fell flat.

Hannah raised her chin in defiance, but the hurt feelings were visible in her eyes. "I don't care if you don't like it," she lied.

"I didn't say I didn't like—"

A ruckus at the door cut off his attempt at recovery as Laura Deane and her good friend Rhonda came in loaded down with boxes. He lunged to take one from Rhonda and sat it down on the desk.

"Oh," she gasped, "what a nice fellow you are." Hannah rolled her eyes and opened it with a pair of scissors.

Luke poked his nose in the box, which was full of little bags with labels like, 'Sleepy' and 'Busy'.

"What's all this?"

"It's not your concern," Hannah sniffed, "but I'm starting a new program to showcase local artists and practitioners."

She directed his attention to some shelves near the center of the room filled with books about art and magic. "Laura makes therapeutic teas, among other things." Hannah planned to fill in around the books with items provided by the town's artisans.

His eyes widened with recognition when Laura extended her hand to introduce herself. Laura Deane and her sister Sarah were known throughout Chuparosa to be powerful witches. There was even talk of them being connected in some way to an angel, and one not necessarily from Heaven.

Before she retired and Hannah took her place, Rhonda Deschene was the town's librarian. Though not as powerful, Rhonda was a natural witch herself who, by all accounts, was like a second mother to the Deane sisters.

He'd never met them before and it could have been his imagination, but the air around the women seemed to crackle. It could also have been Hannah's irritation with him that he was picking up on but either way Luke was intrigued.

He took a cellophane bag from the box. It was filled with dried oranges, cloves, cinnamon sticks, and star anise. She'd labeled it 'Homey' and, according to the tag, the mixture was good for protection.

"Protection?" he wondered aloud.

"With the right intention," Laura explained, "you could use it to drive away negativity and give your space a little bit of a reset."

"How much is this?"

"It's a library," Hannah sighed.

"So, there's no charge," Laura said with a smile. Concerned by his interest in protection, she closed his hand around the bag and said, "Take it and let me know what you think."

When Hannah crossed her arms, he knew he'd worn out his welcome, such as it was, so he left, forgetting his library card and books.

"He's good looking." Laura raised her eyebrows when he'd gone. "I think he likes you."

"He's a menace," Hannah huffed, "and besides, I'm sure he gets plenty of other women with those...those hands and..." she swallowed hard, "that stupid, crooked smile."

"You're right." Laura laughed. "He's probably dreadful. Rhonda, we should hex him."

"I think your man may have a problem." Rhonda called them over to the table where Luke had been sitting.

"He's a problem alright, but he's *not* my man," Hannah reminded them. "I would love to walk around for one day with all that audacity. On top of everything else, look how he left these books scattered around."

"Hmmm." Laura flipped the pages in a book about destructive hauntings. "That simmer pot won't protect him from something that's already in his house."

Hannah closed another book he'd left open titled, 'Haunted Humans'. "You won't have to hex him if he's dealing with this."

Laura's instructions for the simmer pot were easy

enough and the next morning Luke dumped the contents in a saucepan and covered them with water. He was to think back to a time when he felt safe and happy while giving the mixture a stir every now and then.

Penny hovered over the stove, unsure of what to make of Luke's feelings and the sweet-smelling brew. The best memory he had leapt to the forefront of his mind as if it were only days ago when he paid off his small business loan to make Shepherd Construction his own. He'd felt so accomplished after working harder than he ever imagined possible, and he'd never been happier since writing that check.

A grin spread across his face, and he turned his attention to the red peppers and escarole he'd purchased to prepare for the jackrabbit's full moon feast that night. Penny found herself lulled into near sedation by his joyful energy until his thoughts wandered to when, shortly after he paid off the loan, Trudy had him served with divorce papers at a job site in Flagstaff. He pushed away the jolt of sadness, but not before it shook Penny from her peaceful trance.

He leaned over the boiling pot and breathed in deeply. Whether it worked or not, it sure smelled good, and he made a mental note to give Laura an order for more. Hannah might despise him, but her idea to showcase the locals was already working. He cringed thinking of their encounter in the library, and loneliness filled his heart once again.

Penny could no longer tolerate his roller coaster of emotions and when he turned back to the cutting board, the vegetables were brown with rot.

"God dammit," he swore and scraped them in the

trash. "What do you want from me?" He scanned the kitchen and listened hard for an answer but all he heard was Penny humming her song, pleased to be back in familiar angry territory.

He took a backpack from the hall closet, stuffed it with water bottles and granola bars, put on his Diamondbacks cap and left with a slam of the door. The fire still burned under the forgotten simmer pot, but Penny was suspicious of the contents and turned it off.

Luke lived within walking distance of the waterfall trailhead and, as Drew promised, was disheartened thirty minutes later when he came upon a thin drizzle leaking over some rocks. It had just rained so there was more water than he expected, but it sprinkled down to a shallow, murky pool floating with tourist trash.

There was what looked like a connecting trail on the other side of the pool, so he waded across and, after trudging up several well camouflaged switchbacks, reached the edge of a narrow canyon. Though he followed the canyon, the trail was poorly marked from that point on and after another mile or so, he took a bad step.

His cross trainers had done him proud until then, but even a good pair of hiking boots would have struggled to grab on to the loose rocks that rolled under his feet and brought him down hard on his backside.

Drew was right and he shouldn't have gone by himself because he was lost, and no one knew he was out there. It would have been considerably worse if he'd hit his head but, as it was, he hadn't hurt much more than his pride. With a wheeze, he hauled himself up and set about flicking the tiny sharp rocks out of his palms. Blood pooled at his wrist from a gash at the base of his thumb which, after a few one-handed fails, he wrapped loosely in a bandana.

It seemed then like a great time for a break, so he leaned against the mountain and took in the breathtaking desert view. Across the valley, several Mule Deer nibbled at fresh sprouts of green grasses and yellow wildflowers, taking advantage of growth from the recent surprise autumn rains. Lost or not, he was annoyed with himself for not venturing out there sooner.

"Do you see the deer?"

He would be convinced for the rest of his life that his heart actually stopped beating when the soft voice at his back came out of nowhere. He spun around to see Hannah Banks, of all people, and very nearly coded again.

"What are you doing out here?" He gasped.

She put her hands on her hips. "I hike to get away from things that stress me out, but I guess that's not in my cards today."

"Do I stress you out?" His lopsided smile both infuriated her and melted her heart but before she could think of a snarky response, she spotted the blood dripping from his thumb.

"Oh my god, you're bleeding." She snatched his hand in hers and pulled back the cloth to inspect the wound. "This bandana is gross. Don't you have a first aid kit with you?"

He shook his head. "It's not that bad."

"Until it gets infected." She dug around in her pack and then proceeded to clean and dress his cut as well as the scrapes on his palms.

He would have relished the attention if not for the

acid-like burning sensation inflicted by her antiseptic spray. "Don't you have Bactine or something?"

"How is it that the strongest men are always the biggest babies?" The way his chest swelled made it clear that he'd only heard the first part of her sentence, so she finished bandaging his cuts and followed up with a larger criticism. "I guess I don't have to tell you that you should buy some boots You're going to break your leg in those gym shoes."

"Noted," he said, rolling his eyes.

She ignored his sass and stuck her foot out. "This is my favorite brand."

His gaze traveled from the shoe along the muscles in her calf up to the hem of her shorts that stopped a little less than halfway down her thigh. "Nice."

"Ugh." She pushed past him. "Have a good hike."

"Thanks for the first aid!" he called after her, then remembered he was still lost and ran to catch up. "Look, I don't know these mountains very well so if you'll point me to the waterfall, I'll get out of your hair."

"You didn't bring a trail map?"

"No."

"What exactly is in your backpack?"

"Water and granola bars."

She blinked at him, surprised he hadn't already died of stupidity. Hannah was from Chuparosa and knew that their location wasn't on a map anyway. That made her responsible for keeping him safe and on their Side of the veil.

She heaved a dramatic sigh and said, "This way leads back to my pickup."

They hadn't noticed the two bobcats tracking them along the ridge above. They didn't see the rattlesnake on the side of the path either, but they both heard it's warning at the same time. Hannah turned in a panicked circle.

"Where is it?" She'd no sooner said the words than the snake struck and one of the bobcats jumped down in front of them, skidding across the snake's path and upsetting its aim.

"Give it a minute to calm down and I'm sure it will go away," Hannah sputtered.

"Are you serious?" Luke's voice was a bit higher of an octave than he was used to, but from what he could tell she was talking to the bobcat.

"He must be from the Other Side, or he wouldn't be helping us. Luke, Chuparosa has a way of taking care of its own."

The bobcat swatted at the snake, all coiled up and ready to strike again. The second bobcat chose then to join his brother in the battle and after the day he'd already had it was two bobcats and one rattlesnake more than Luke could handle.

Hannah reached out to steady him, but he shouted, "Look out! There's two!" Though he stretched his arms wide to shield her, he knocked Hannah off balance and over the cliff.

She tumbled about ten feet before splashing down on a wide rock formation full of rainwater that protruded from the side of the mountain.

"Hold still! I'm coming to get you!"

She looked up to see Luke flanked on each side by a bobcat, all three of them looking at each other and then peering down at her.

"Unbelievable," she muttered. Then her breathing grew shallow and quick as she gaped at the cavernous expanse under the rocks.

Luke could see her panic rising. "Hannah!" he shouted, "don't look down! Look at me!" He started over the side with nothing to hold on to and she was convinced that he was going to fall.

"There's rope in my backpack!" she called to him.

He stopped his descent and then disappeared over the top, leaving the bobcats to stand guard. Minutes later, one end of the rope slapped down to the rock. He wrapped the other end around his waist and leaned back as she climbed.

Once he'd heaved her over the side, she scrambled away from the edge. "Where's the snake?"

When Luke pointed to a limp coil in the dirt, she tilted her head accusingly at the bobcats. "Did you do that?"

They seemed quite pleased with themselves, each taking half a snake before leaping to the top of the ridge and sprinting off to eat their breakfast.

Luke gagged a little and then helped Hannah to her feet. There were deep scratches all over her limbs and the cut on her knee had reopened. Her t-shirt was shredded, and dozens of cactus spines poked out from her socks.

Without thinking he pulled her close and said, "Jesus, Hannah. I'm so sorry." Her body stiffened in his embrace, so he let her go, apologized again and backed away.

"I know it was an accident, I'm just—" She could feel the tears welling up in her eyes and covered her face with her hands.

Unsure what to do next, he looked around for the hoodie that had been tied around her waist but found it clinging to a prickly pear several feet below them. An unfamiliar sense of helplessness overtook him and in desperation he blurted, "Do you want a granola bar?"

Her shoulders began to shake with what he thought were sobs, but she turned her face up to him laughing through her tears.

"You idiot," she blubbered and rested her forehead against his chest. When he held her that time, she relaxed into his arms.

The trek to her pickup was slow and then he drove them to his house. It was her intent to drop him off and leave but she was still quite shaky and he was uncomfortable letting her get behind the wheel.

"Come inside and let me take care of you." He dropped her keys in his pocket and since she didn't have the strength to wrestle him for them, she nodded quietly and let him lead her inside.

Just over the threshold, she stopped short in surprise. "Your house smells amazing."

"You can thank Laura Deane for that."

She remembered what he'd been reading in the library the day Laura gave him the potion and looked around uneasily. "About those books..."

He didn't really want to talk about his poltergeist, but he couldn't be sure that it wouldn't cause trouble while Hannah was there, so he thought it best to at least warn her. First, he took her to the bathroom, presented her with some towels and a long flannel shirt, then excused himself.

Looking in the mirror, she was horrified by her matted hair and the dirt streaks on her face that marked the tracks of her tears.

The only real improvement she could see after a

shower was that she was clean, but his breath caught in his throat when she emerged from the bathroom wearing nothing but the shirt he'd given her. Her own shirt was trashed, but he offered to wash the rest of her soaking wet clothes.

Hannah paused in the laundry room, asking, "Where is that music coming from?"

Penny was suspicious of the new woman and hummed her song loudly in protest of Hannah's presence. Luke sighed and opened the washer.

"This house is haunted." He put in her clothes, braced his hands on the rim of the machine and continued, "I thought I could handle it on my own, but it seems to be getting worse."

Penny took offense to his claim and slammed the lid closed, catching his fingers underneath it.

Hannah jumped away from the machine. "Good god!"

"See what I mean?" He winced and pulled his hands free.

"You can't get rid of it until you find out who it is." She followed him to the kitchen where he put the kettle on for tea.

"How am I supposed to do that?"

He left briefly and returned with a bottle of Bactine and some cotton balls. She watched his steady hands dab at her deepest cuts and caught herself wondering what they would feel like on the rest of her body.

"I am a librarian, Luke. I know how to find information."

He finished up and she left the kitchen chair for the couch, though the move was more to gather her composure than to rest.

Looking around, she noticed with approval that he hadn't turned feral after his divorce. It was a clean, custom house that he was obviously proud of, full of architectural details that put his skill and personality on display. The exposed wooden beams in the ceiling gave the place a rustic look that she particularly loved.

He handed her a cup of tea, flipped the switch to turn on the fireplace, and pulled a chenille throw blanket from the back of the couch to cover her bare legs. "Are you sure you're alright?"

She nodded; grateful he hadn't noticed the shiver that went through her when his fingers grazed her thigh.

He flopped next to her and let his head fall back against the couch while he went over the wild events of the week in his head.

He jerked awake to find the late afternoon sun poking through the blinds and Hannah asleep on his shoulder. His mind raced. She'd been kind of sweet to him before he pushed her off the cliff. Could he be so lucky that she actually had feelings for him?

Her eyes fluttered open as he brushed the hair from her face and she couldn't believe it, but her first instinct was to snuggle up to him. Despite their rather rough encounters, she'd never worried for her safety around him, yet beyond that she had no idea how he would respond to an advance from her.

The possible scenarios played out in her head, and, at worst, he simply wasn't attracted to her. They would have an awkward and humiliating exchange, about which she would never tell a soul, and then they would spend the rest of their lives avoiding each other in town. At best, well, she didn't dare think about that, and curled into his chest before losing her nerve.

Without hesitation, he wrapped her in his arms and murmured, "God, you feel good."

She lifted her chin to meet his eyes and he slid his fingers into her hair, pulling gently on her head to bring their lips together. Her mouth was so soft, and the way she melted into him strained the edges of his self-control. He laid her back on the couch, and she felt him grow hard against her as his tongue found hers. He undid a button on the flannel shirt and whispered, "Do you want me?"

She arched into him and then, in a scenario Hannah never could have predicted, Luke's ex-wife rang the doorbell.

"Oh no," he groaned and dropped his head on her chest. "I forgot Trudy was coming over to pick up the decorations."

Hannah's emotions took a lightning-fast ride from passion to panic, but then she gathered herself up, rebuttoned the flannel and sighed, "Meeting your ex is just one of a long list of things I wasn't counting on today." She ignored his pained expression and gestured to the door. "I can't wait to see what happens next."

Unlike Trudy, Hannah had at least been given a few seconds notice before their meeting and when Luke went to the garage for the decorations, she did her best to keep the mood polite and decent, even as she stood there wearing next to nothing.

Trudy paced the living room, inspecting Luke's new décor. She'd taken almost everything when she moved out and hadn't expected him to cobble together as much style on his own. He'd gone with dark blue furniture and, insomuch as there were accents, they tended to be either hunter green or brown, giving the house more of a log cabin feel which was accentuated by the fireplace.

The fireplace she'd never really wanted. The fireplace that was burning in front of the rumpled couch with its pillows strewn under the coffee table where two mugs sat cooling near the bruised up, half-naked woman standing in front of her.

Trudy's cheeks burned. "This is so like him," she fumed, "not thinking of anyone but himself."

"Believe me," Hannah said, raising her hands in defense, "I would be furious right now, but this has been a very strange week and I'm not surprised he forgot that you were coming over."

"Oh, but it's always something," Trudy cautioned. "You'll plan a trip for your birthday, but he'll get a job in Tucson that week." She folded the blanket with what Hannah thought was excessive force and let her warning become a tell-all as she tossed it on the recliner.

"It was exciting when he started his own business until he moved me out here to the boondocks and went from working sixty hours a week to a hundred." She plucked the throw pillows from the floor, punched them into shape and arranged them on the couch.

"I spent all my time trying to get back at him and when we weren't fighting," Trudy narrowed her eyes, hoping to scare the new woman off in a final act of revenge, "he had...erectile dysfunction."

Luke stood frozen out of sight in the hallway, holding the box of decorations and wishing the poltergeist would drag him through the wood floor straight into Hell. Then Hannah surprised him again.

She could sympathize, and the divorce must have

been awful for both of them, but it was none of her business. If you'd asked her the day before, she would have sworn that she was not one to engage in petty fights over a man. However, Trudy had taken an unnecessary cheap shot at Luke. Since falling off the cliff that morning, Hannah found that there were plenty of depths to which she would more willingly sink.

She made a show of adjusting the flannel shirt and said, "He has no problem getting it up for me."

Luke's mouth fell open and he barged into the room. "Here's your stuff." He nodded toward the front door. "Go open your trunk."

He followed a scowling Trudy outside and Hannah stood rigid by the coffee table with her hands over her mouth until the song of Samsung echoed through the house, jolting her out of her thoughts with its notification that her clothes were ready.

Penny was confused when Luke went outside and blamed Hannah for his departure. She jerked on her hair and then chased her from the laundry room by throwing every item she could reach until Hannah took shelter behind the recliner.

"Get down!" she screamed when Luke came back.

He dropped to his knees in the entryway as a lamp smashed against the door, just missing his head. He crawled to her, shielding her with his body as a bar stool flew across the room and crashed into them.

"Stop!" he shouted to the air, but Penny was beyond reason and slashed at him with a steak knife she'd lifted from the dish drain. He used a fireplace poker to bat the knife out of the air and wiped at the blood running down his arms. "Jesus," He swore in disbelief.

"You can't stay here, Luke," Hannah panted.

He took her by the hand and led her to the bedroom, dodging their tea mugs and then the entire coffee table.

"Hurry," she begged as he stuffed some of his things in a gym bag.

He zipped up the bag, opened the bedroom window and pushed out the screen. He gave her a boost and then climbed out after her as Penny hurled everything from his nightstand after them.

Ducking away from an unabridged hard cover copy of The Stand, they ran to their vehicles and Hannah hollered, "Follow me home and we'll figure this out!"

"That thing nearly opened a vein." Hannah cringed, taking her first aid kit from the cabinet. "It seems like I just bandaged you up a little while ago. Oh wait, I did. Or was it you bandaging me?"

Luke perched on a stool in her kitchen while she wrapped up his forearm. He brushed his hand over the gashes she'd received on her trip off the cliff side and said, "I guess we're running at about even right now."

"This is not a race to the death." Remembering the bar stool, she lifted his t-shirt and gingerly touched his ribs. "Anything broken?"

"I doubt it." He so enjoyed having her hands on him that he couldn't have felt a broken bone if there was one.

Their stomachs had been rumbling for a while, so she scanned her fridge for something quick and the chicken she roasted the day before gave her an idea. "Do you want a quesadilla?"

He nodded, his mouth watering at the suggestion.

"I'm sure you could use this too." She handed him a beer.

"Like you wouldn't believe."

Tossing his beer cap in the trash bin under the sink, he noticed that it had recently been resealed. He eyed a sizeable dribble of caulk dried to the faucet and fumed to himself, wondering what kind of asshole would take advantage of a widow by doing such sloppy work.

"Who did your sink?"

"I did," she said proudly. "I learned how on YouTube." Catching his expression she added, "Why? What's wrong with it?"

"Nothing," he backtracked, "you did a good job."

"Not really," she acknowledged, picking at the dried glob, "but I tried."

Hannah's house was one of the oldest in Chuparosa, but it was charming, and she told him that it belonged to her parents before they passed away. Looking around, he saw more than a few other broken things. Some, like the sink, she'd worked on herself. The rest she had either not gotten around to or figured she could live with. It would only take him a few hours to fix it all, but he decided to keep his mouth shut until a more appropriate time.

She brought her laptop to the table and, as they ate, searched back issues of the Chuparosa Chronicle for deaths in the area. There was an unsettling number of them, but only a few caught her eye. The fatal accident of a tourist in the mountains a year earlier, the death of a young girl on the highway near the entrance of his development, and the murder of an abusive man by his wife—they'd found his body in a shallow grave ten years later when Desert Falls first broke ground.

"Don't these sound like they would make good hauntings to you?" She sat back in her chair and rubbed her neck. "We should see if there's anything Sheriff Ruiz can tell us about them tomorrow."

"Hannah, I can't thank you enough. You showing up for me like this goes above and beyond anything I could have imagined possible."

She stood for a full body stretch and then bent to kiss his cheek. "You're growing on me."

He pulled her onto his lap and kissed her deeply. "We started something earlier that I'd really like to finish, if we weren't so..." his voice trailed off.

She traced his lips with her fingers and completed his sentence, "If we weren't so damn tired."

She took some Ibuprofen, handed him the bottle, and showed him to the shower before falling into bed. She didn't stir when he slid in next to her and once his head hit the pillow, he too was sound asleep.

She hadn't remembered to close the blinds, so they woke together with the sunrise. He stroked her hair and whispered, "Good morning," in her ear.

She looked up with a sleepy smile and asked, "How do you feel?"

"How do I feel?" He propped himself on an elbow. "I woke up with you in my arms, wearing my shirt, looking sexy as hell." He pulled their hips together. "Hannah, I feel great."

Emboldened by his encouragement, she rained kisses along his jaw and then nibbled his earlobe before returning her mouth to his, sucking lightly on his bottom lip.

"God," Sparks of passion flashed in his eyes. "You don't know what you do to me." His kisses were hungry, but his calloused hands were gentle as they moved down her throat to unbutton the flannel shirt. She arched her neck against the pillow, savoring the feel of him, and made a soft noise when his tongue swirled around her nipples and his fingers explored farther below.

"Luke," she whispered, and buried her hands in his hair, "I want you."

He shed his pajama pants and slipped between her legs, growling low as he eased himself into her.

"How do you want me?"

"Slow," she whispered.

He synchronized the movement of his hips to their languid kisses, and she traced her fingers up and down his spine when they found their rhythm. Her grip tightened as the intensity of her pleasure built up until finally her nails raked down his back and she wrapped her legs around him, crying out his name. His body tensed and he thrust harder and harder until he lost control, collapsing with a groan in her arms.

As their breathing slowed, he pressed himself onto his side, gave her his crooked smile, and playfully repeated her question back to her. "How do *you* feel?"

"Hopeful."

Though her response was confident, he couldn't help but notice the nervousness in her smile. He would have to choose his next words carefully, so he rolled on to his back and lay quietly for a long moment.

She pulled the sheet to her chin and inched away from him. Could she have been so wrong about his intentions? Dread squeezed around her heart, and then he reached for her.

"Look at me." He lifted her chin until their eyes met. "I'm not playing with you. We got off to a rough start, but you know as well as I do there's something special happening between us and I'd like to see how far we can take it."

His sweet words caught her completely off guard. Thrilled, yet irritated, she narrowed her eyes and pushed him in the chest. "I thought you were going to dump me."

He blinked at her. "What?"

"You hesitated so long."

He rubbed his temples and sighed, "I was trying to pick words that wouldn't scare you away."

"Luke, if pushing me off a cliff before taking me to your haunted house to meet your angry ex-wife didn't scare me away, nothing will." She took his face in her hands and pressed her forehead to his. "Because you're right, there is something special between us."

He let out a long exhale and kissed the tip of her nose. "Then we should celebrate that great sex with our first date. If you let me buy you breakfast at Racine's, I promise not to get us killed on the way. Afterward," he said with a wink, "I'll take you to look at those death files."

"You," she laughed, "are a hopeless romantic."

"Here you go." Sheriff Ruiz tossed three thin folders on his desk. "You two were lucky to get out of there alive."

Luke studied the evidence surrounding the case of the murdered wife beater. "My money's on this guy." He tried to show Hannah the details, but she shook her head without looking up from the file in her hand.

"Penny Poole was a pop star," she said to herself, then opened the music streaming app on her phone.

After a quick search she pressed play and turned up the volume for the men to hear. "Sound familiar?"

"Oh my god." Luke shuddered. "That's it." He turned to Chuck. "That's the song the ghost hums in my house."

"It was her one hit." Hannah's eyes reddened. "The poor baby was seventeen when she died on that road with her whole life ahead of her."

"That would piss me off too, but why is she acting out now?" Chuck wondered. "She rolled her car in the eighties."

"We need to talk to Laura Deane," Luke said.

"Sorry man." Chuck shrugged his shoulders. "She went to Sedona with Sebastian Scott."

Hannah stared out the window, tapping a finger on her chin until she noticed Rhonda on the sidewalk outside. "I have an idea." She jumped up and ran out the door.

"And there she goes," Luke sighed. "Can you believe she never batted an eyelash about any of this?"

"Careful," Chuck warned, "you might find yourself in love with a good woman."

Luke handed him the file. "She's either going to be my everything or she's going to ruin my life."

"Would it change anything if you knew which it was gonna be?"

"No." Luke's gaze followed her out the window. "In fact, I'd relive all of it, over and over."

Chuck's eyes darted around the room. "Don't give Chuparosa any ideas, man."

"Rhonda has offered to help us," Hannah said as Luke

trotted out to meet them.

"Should we get a Ouija board or something?" he asked, figuring the local grocery market probably carried them.

"You don't want to do that, honey," Rhonda warned. "Without protection, you'll give yourself spiritual crabs."

Luke made a face. "So how do we get rid of her."

"I don't know if we should do that either," Hannah said carefully. "She's a teenager who just needs a little redirection."

"Redirection to where?"

Both women looked toward the library. "Where we can look after her."

"No way, Hannah." Luke stomped his foot. "I can't let you do that."

"Good thing you're not the boss of me." She turned on her heel and crossed the street.

"Where is she going?" Luke was exasperated. "I drove us here."

"Penny is more dangerous in your house. She's a lonely child who needs to be around others like her."

"Of course." He hung his head, grossed out by the inference. "Not a single, middle-aged man."

Rhonda gave him sympathetic look. "It's not your fault, but you can help her."

They found Hannah leaning stubbornly against his Silverado and after a quick stop at Rhonda's house for supplies, they were back in his driveway.

"Oh, my word," Rhonda gasped.

All the front windows were busted out from the inside and the rooms looked like they'd been tossed by the FBI.

"Penny?" Hannah and Rhonda called out to her as they crunched through the glass in the doorway. "Penny Poole?"

"Careful." Luke stayed close, watching them and surveying the considerable damage to his home. How in the world was he going to explain it to the insurance company? Penny picked up on his frustration and soon her song echoed through the house. "There she is."

Rhonda wasted no time and handed them each a bundle of what looked a little like Baby's Breath tied up with twine into thick wands. "I normally use Boneset to draw out fevers, but it will draw out spirits too."

Hannah called to her again, but Penny recognized the voice of the woman who left with Luke and threw plates at her from the kitchen.

"Penny, no!" Luke scolded.

Rhonda lit their wands and pungent smoke filled the air. "Get her to follow you, Luke."

He stood in the middle of the kitchen, hoping she was nearby and waved the Boneset over his head. Unable to help herself, Penny hovered so near to him that he could feel her presence.

He was not a father but in the authoritative tone so natural to some men, he said, "Penny, it's not safe for you here so I'm taking you to a better place."

She swirled around, gathered pieces of broken glass and used them to dig in the walls. At first, they thought she was just doing more damage but then Rhonda said, "No honey, it won't be like that."

Luke took a step back and his eyes reddened as he read the single word she'd scratched into the wall:
A L O N E.

"I'll be there almost every day," Hannah assured

her, "and Luke will come to visit, and you'll be surrounded by kids your own age."

Surrounded? Penny hadn't seen a young person in over thirty years and she wondered what sort of place it could be. Luke felt her excitement as she zipped impatiently around his head, so he slowly walked his smoke wand to the front door where she followed him out.

Flanked by Rhonda and Hannah, he led Penny into town.

"Are you sure she's with us?" Hannah wondered.

Luke nodded. "I can feel her."

He thought they must look like they'd lost their minds but in Chuparosa people don't ask questions they don't really want the answers to, so they were left unbothered to complete their task.

In the library, they piled their burning Boneset in a large dish Hannah placed on a table near the young adult section. Penny flittered around upsetting displays and flinging armfuls of books to the floor until a copy of the Hunger Games fell open and caught her attention. She read those two pages, soared through the shelves some more and then returned to the book, flipping to chapter one.

Hannah sprinkled ghost shaped confetti over the round table and stood back to admire her Halloween display. She'd included books for all ages about ghosts and spirits of all kinds, enlisting Penny's help to make sure the young adult selections weren't lame.

In a short time, Penny had learned that she could relate to the feelings of the characters in a good story and didn't rely as much on the emotions of others to cover up her own pain. Teenagers flocked to the library since they learned it was haunted and the number of young readers in town nearly doubled.

"I really like the display." Luke came up behind her and wrapped his arms around her waist, sheepishly asking, "Are you mad? I think we can still make the reservation."

They'd had dinner plans, but he ran late at work. In those days being late was a rare occurrence for him and her only real concern was the traffic in Phoenix. They would never make it across town in time. She packed up her things and pitched him a new plan.

"Why don't we have a burger at Isaac's tonight and wait for the weekend to go to the city."

Penny nudged them together again and Luke pulled Hannah close, realizing then that he was in fact in love with a good woman and finally understanding how Chuparosa takes care of its own.

The following is only Chuparosa adjacent, but I forgive myself because I loved Doug and Angie so much that they started showing up in the Deane witch series. After a visit to one of Arizona's many quirky little towns, I am positive that this could have happened, but it is not a true story.

Fire Resistance

She knew what he was doing. Jeff had been working ridiculously hard to manage an ever more complicated stream of bullshit, but Angela had found out about Megan months ago. That he *could* have a woman on the side occurred to her the morning he tore up their apartment insisting he didn't need her help in the search for his lost cell phone.

That he *did* have a woman on the side was confirmed when the phone tumbled out of a laundry basket with the dirty clothes she was preparing to wash. As she called out to let him know, a text notification from someone named Megan Tanner appeared and the first line read: `Sorry about last night.`

She thought he'd been unreasonably grumpy when

an alleged gathering with his buddies was abruptly cancelled the night before. Though he accepted Angela's offer to cancel her own plans so they could be together, Jeff fell into a horrible mood and ended up sulking and drinking in front of the television. The phone must have fallen in the basket as he stumbled around getting ready for bed.

Her initial inclination was to hurl it at him and storm out in a huff of self-righteous indignation, never to lay eyes on the miserable bastard again. The royalty checks from the books she wrote didn't even cover her car insurance bill though, and she was in between freelancing jobs. Funds were tight to say the least and, as far as she knew, she and Jeff were still moving up north together.

He'd just bought his dream house in a tiny northern Arizona town and the chance to escape the heat and chaos of Phoenix to write amidst the pine trees was too delicious to pass up. So rather than pull back, she leaned into their relationship, doting on him and excitedly making plans for the next chapter of their lives together.

She was hurt but had to admit that Jeff had never been Mr. Wonderful. The more she thought about it, he was barely Mr. This Will Do For Now, and she'd been too lazy to address it. For the most part, he treated her well so she'd ignored the dozen or so red flags that he'd been waving all long in favor of good sex and financial support. She shuddered to think about what he would have to say about her, yet at some point along the way, they'd made a silent agreement to settle for one another.

In truth, Megan had done them both a service and she could have him without a fight as long as she waited until after the move. Angela decided to take a calculated risk, assuming that Jeff wouldn't end things first and that she could get out with grace after finding a job and a place of her own in their new town.

It soon became clear to her that Megan didn't necessarily want Jeff either. Forty-five minutes of online detective work revealed that Ms. Tanner was a successful marketing executive living in Scottsdale with a short haired cat named Theodore and an obsession with eighties detective shows. She posted pictures every weekend with her friends, but there were no boyfriends on any of her social media accounts—ever. There were, however, plenty of clever feminist memes about remaining single and living life to the fullest.

Part of Angela wanted to hire Megan to help her sell more books but, unable to afford it, she was content to watch Jeff unravel as the other woman led him on. His ever-changing moods gave her emotional whiplash.

When Megan withheld her attention, he couldn't seem to get enough of Angela. He was hedging his bets and it burned her up to be considered his consolation prize. Still, she convinced herself that, in time, she would become resistant to the pain.

When he left her surrounded by boxes in the new house for an impromptu *work trip*, she knew what he was doing then too. She'd intercepted an email in which he begged Megan to talk and to give them a chance. Angela knew he was driving back to the valley for a meeting with her. It was his last-ditch effort and if he failed to win Megan, he would come home and renew their unspoken agreement.

It would be shocking if Megan agreed, given her

behavior up to that point, but Angela no longer cared. She had made it up north and was already at work on her plan.

She turned in circles for a while amidst the mess and then unpacked a box of her unsold books, lovingly arranging them on the empty shelves. The task of setting up the new home might have been exciting except that it wasn't her home, and she was unlikely to be there very long. It was a shame because they both fell in love with the little house and were delighted to learn it was well within Jeff's price range.

There were hard wood floors, a brick fireplace and every window looked out into the forest. The previous owner had even left the round farmhouse kitchen table she'd gushed over. But it was the wraparound porch that sold them on the house before they ever stepped inside. They envisioned afternoons in the back, working on their laptops, and evenings at a bistro table in front, chatting with neighbors holding glasses of wine.

She shook off the sentiment, reminding herself not to get too attached. It would make matters much worse when Jeff returned, announcing that she'd been swapped out for Megan. They had so much in common and she struggled just then to remember when it was that they started simply going through the motions.

If he were willing to commit to her, she might have forgiven a random affair as a wake-up call, and the new location could have been the beginning of a spectacular comeback romance.

The truth was that he didn't want to marry her, or he would have asked; but it didn't upset her that much, or she would have left him. They were both so afraid of being alone that they'd stayed together in a sort of deep relationship sleep.

Still, it sickened her to wonder how many other Megans he'd auditioned for over the years. How close had he gotten to leaving her before? The dreamy little house began to close in on her, so she shoved her laptop in a backpack and raced out the door, pausing on the porch for a few minutes to breathe in the fresh, pine scented air.

Angela made her way on foot to the local coffee shop, ostensibly to work but really to meet some new people. Hoping to make a good impression and maybe even get a lead on a job, she ordered a coffee and arranged herself at a table right by the door. A few patrons stared but most seemed uninterested in the newcomer.

She worked for half an hour or so and then got up to stretch her legs, smiling as she noticed an index card pinned to the bulletin board with the words 'Help Wanted' written in red marker. Her smile widened when she pulled out the thumbtack and read that the local newspaper was in need of a copywriter.

"You're Mrs. Nelson." Angela jumped, dropping the card and sloshing coffee on the floor. A tall woman reached around her, picked up the card, and repined it to the board. "He left for graduate school."

"I'm sorry, what?" Angela snatched a handful of napkins from the counter and knelt to wipe up the mess.

"Terrence was the former reporter's name. He left that job to go to graduate school."

"Oh." Angela tossed the soggy napkins in the trash and tried to compose herself. "It's good to know that he didn't quit on bad terms."

The woman didn't comment on Angela's

supposition but continued with one of her own. "I saw your husband, Mr. Jeffrey Nelson, is it? I saw him leave town this morning. He drives a Jeep."

"He's my boyfriend," Angela stammered. In a town of less than a thousand people, she expected the locals to be in their business, but they'd literally just moved in. "We're not married."

Given how quickly word seemed to get around, she didn't want to give anyone the wrong idea and complicate potential future romances, especially if Megan showed up. She wanted a peaceful transition and a fresh start.

"I'm Angela Walsh, but friends call me Angie." No one had ever called her Angie, but she'd always thought it sounded more happy-go-lucky.

The woman said, "Not married," so loudly that Angie flinched, embarrassed by the sideways glances she received from around the shop.

Cheeks burning, Angie plucked the card from the bulletin board again and left to gather up her things. Maybe it was better to get a job first so the locals would know she was serious about becoming one of them.

Anxious to put the awkward encounter behind her, she shoved open the coffee shop door, nearly knocking a tiny blonde-haired woman off her feet. Apologizing profusely, Angie offered the woman everything from a cup of coffee to an ambulance ride.

"Look at you, just a bundle of nerves." The woman brushed off her apologies and led her to a table. "My name is Elena and I'm just fine. You must be Angela. It's absolutely shameful that I haven't been by your place yet to say hello."

"Call me Angie." Again, she was amazed by the

familiarity since they had only moved in the day before.

"Come and sit with me, Angie."

Angie scanned the room and eyed the tall woman, seated with her back to them at a long counter running down the center of the room. She relaxed a bit but sat on the edge of her chair, ready to run if accosted again. Elena was kind and open and, as they chatted, Angie learned that she was fairly new in town herself. She was the Preacher's wife and they'd just transferred in from southern Arizona. She and Pastor Ryan were already enjoying the cooler weather and looking forward to their first snowy winter in years.

Angie shared the basics of her own story, adding that since she and Jeff could work from anywhere, they chose the most beautiful place they could find. When Elena pressed, she admitted to being an author struggling to find readers and that she was anxious to apply for the copywriter position.

"Well, praise God. That's the perfect job for you. I am a voracious reader, myself. Tell me about your novels."

Angie swallowed hard, reluctant to lose her new friend so quickly. Elena hadn't even blinked after learning she and Jeff weren't married, but there were lines a preacher's wife had to hold.

"I'm in the horror genre. Witchcraft, angels, demons—that sort of thing."

Elena's eyes widened. "How exciting, I just re-read The Witching Hour."

Angie gasped in surprise and Elena laughed, leaning forward with her voice low. "I believe angels and demons exist, my sweet sister, and we should pay attention when creative people like you tell their stories.

Everyone understands the supernatural differently and those distinctive experiences are very important.”

“I’m afraid Anne Rice had more talent in her shift key than I ever will, but I do love to write.”

They talked for a while about other genres and their favorite authors until Angie sat back and confessed sheepishly, “If I’m honest Elena, I’d rather write romance novels. They’re so much fun, but as they say, you should *write what you know.*”

Before Elena could ask how she knew so much about horror, the tall woman looked up from her phone. “Be careful who you’re going around with, ma’am, you shouldn’t be shaming the Preacher when he’s not around.”

Elena said nothing in response but gave her a long, hard stare. When she returned her attention back to Angie, the building rattled as if a large truck had rumbled by. The tall woman’s coffee cup jumped off the table and shattered to the floor, splashing the hot liquid across her sandaled feet. She leapt up with a yelp and snapped her fingers at the young barista, who sprinted around the counter with a towel.

Unbothered, Elena rose and said, “I’d better let you go since you have a job to apply for. Will we see you in church on Sunday?”

“I don’t go to church.” Angie tensed for Elena’s response but was met only with a warm smile.

“Then Ryan and I will visit you when Jeff gets home.”

On her way to the newspaper office, she pulled out her phone to call Jeff, but then remembered why he was gone and changed her mind. It made her sad and she would miss having him to talk to, but Megan would likely disapprove of any contact between them. Thoughts of Megan made her angry and she changed her mind again, hoping he would feel guilty when she called. There was tension in his voice, and he obviously wasn't listening to her.

"What do you care if the Preacher's wife is mean and weird?" He asked absently.

"No, Elena is very nice—never mind. When are you coming home?"

"I'm going to my mom's house for the weekend and then I'll drive back up there on Monday."

"Monday? Jeff, it's only Thursday!"

"Leave the unpacking and go for a hike or something. I'll help you next week. I promise." He paused for a moment, finally giving her his full attention. "Angela, I really do promise, and you know I miss you."

So, Megan had turned him down. She hung up and clutched the phone to her heart. A part of her had longed to hear words like, *I miss you* from him for so long that it startled her and brought tears to her eyes when he said them. He would be coming home to her, but if Megan had loved him back, Angela would be yesterday's news and the tears in her eyes spilled over her cheeks.

"Trouble in paradise?"

She spun around to find a grubby, sweaty man looking her up and down as he heaved several boxes in to the bed of his truck. She wiped her face with her hands and realized that she'd wandered in front of the hardware store.

"Were you listening to my phone call?"

"You're standing in the middle of the sidewalk, so I didn't really have a choice. If I were you though, I'd keep my private business to myself. All of it."

He was a few inches taller than her, with blonde hair and a scruffy beard that had enough gray in it to make him look a little older than she suspected he was. She surmised that it had taken years of doing manual labor for him to be able to make the task of moving those heavy boxes seem so effortless. She jumped when he slammed the tailgate and he smirked, resting a finger on his lips to emphasize the warning he'd given her.

"I'm trying, but I'd also like to make friends." She stuck out her hand. "Angela Walsh—Angie."

"Doug Farmer." He put on a dusty baseball cap, tipping the brim at her. "Listen, this town is even smaller than it looks, so take care." He managed a tight smile as he climbed in his truck but there was something dark in his eyes that made her shudder on his behalf.

She arrived at the newspaper office just as the editor flipped the 'Closed' sign in the window and decided to call it a day.

At home she slipped on a pair of Jeff's sweatpants and curled up on the couch with her laptop and a glass of wine. It was the only bottle in the house, and she had a feeling that it would be hard to find a new one in town.

Sipping slowly, she opened a new document and by 2am found that she'd written four thousand words about a farmer named Doug who also happened to be a werewolf. The Doug in her story had managed for years to keep his secret until falling in love with Ashley, the beautiful and mysterious reporter who just moved to town.

Smiling to herself, she scrolled through the pages. The story was fun and it was nice, for a change, to write about the nuances of a make-believe werewolf relationship instead of the terrifying reality of religious trauma. Thinking about her novels, she logged in to her sales reports and was pleasantly surprised to find two new eBook sales. She poured herself another glass of wine to celebrate and returned to the adventures of Doug and Ashley.

Just before dawn she was startled by a loud, sharp knock at the door. Peeking through the curtain, she saw nothing on the porch but a large rock with a rubber band around it. She opened the door and ran her fingers along a new dent in the wood before quickly slamming it shut. She turned on every light in the house but the shadows cast by the boxes appeared to slide around the room, only adding to her unease.

What she didn't know was that a piece of paper had slipped from under the rubber band when the rock was thrown. The wind blew it across the yard and Angie never saw the note, but scrawled in hateful letters was the word 'whore'.

Despite having a sleepless night, she stopped by the newspaper office first thing in the morning. The editor sighed heavily when she walked in and handed him the index card from the bulletin board.

"I'd like to apply for this job."

He gave her back the card and said, "I don't need a novelist."

Town gossip was travelling at the speed of light, but she was undeterred. "I'm a freelance writer and I'll give you my website address if you'd like to see my work."

"I've seen your work," he sniffed. "Demons and witches aren't suitable for this paper."

"There are angels too." She tried not to sound defensive, understanding that her novels weren't everyone's cup of tea. If sales were any indicator, they were hardly anyone's cup of tea, but she'd also written articles on everything from lifeguard training to cotton farming with no mention of witchcraft at all.

"Look, I'm more than qualified to do this and I really need a job. I promise to write only what you tell me to."

He looked around as if someone were watching them. "Get me five hundred words on the new preacher."

"Pastor Ryan?"

"The town's not too sure about him yet, so see what you can find out. I'll pay you for the article, but I'm not making any promises beyond that."

Angie was elated. She could write a puff piece on the new preacher in her sleep but was determined to make it her best work ever. Anything to impress that editor enough to give her the job.

She left the office and headed to the coffee shop for a celebratory cinnamon latte, but the tall woman was standing out front talking to Doug. She turned an about face, but the woman had seen her and called out, "I saw your Instagram and all that witchy trash."

Angie faced them, tiring of the woman's snarkiness and snapped, "I write books about witches, so my social media accounts are filled with fun, magical things for my fans." If she had any fans, she was sure that they would love it.

"Trash."

Angie folded her arms across her chest. "Well, it's not for everyone."

The tall woman shot Doug a look and stomped away.

"So, you got a job," he said.

"I literally just left the office. How could you possibly—" She shook her head and gave up on the question, deciding instead to get to work. "My editor wants an article on Pastor Ryan. Have you met him?

"I go to church." His tone was sharp and defensive.

"I...I just thought you might know him personally. I've met his wife, Elena, but I'm looking for some additional insight before I talk to the man himself."

"I won't be part of a smear campaign against anyone."

"What?" She laughed. "It's just fluff so people can feel like they know him a little better."

"Hmph. I'm sure that's what he told you. Be careful how you make a living, Angie." Doug's voice was harsher than he'd intended it to be, so he added, more softly, "I'm just trying to help you out."

There were mud clumps on his boots, a grease smear across his cheek, and he was covered head to toe in a fine film of red dust. He was probably dirty all the time because of his work, but he kept dusting off his jeans as if all of a sudden he was aware of that fact.

"You're full of warnings, aren't you?" She picked a pine needle out of his collar. "What do *you* do for a living?"

He waved a hand proudly over the sign on his truck

that read 'Farmer Forest Management' and said, "You'll have to clear all that dead brush around your place before fire season."

"I suppose you're the only forest manager in town?" she teased.

"I'll send you a quote." He grinned for a just a second before he caught himself and she was stunned by how the smile lit up his eyes.

Another question occurred to her as he turned to leave. "Hey, what college did Terrence go to?"

"College?" He frowned.

"The tall woman said he left the newspaper to go to grad school."

Doug's eyes narrowed. "If that's what she said, then that's what happened."

"Ms. Walsh?"

She no longer jumped out of her skin when people snuck up on her and she somehow knew right away who the tender, kind voice in her ear belonged to.

"Pastor Ryan, I've been looking for you."

Doug slammed the door of his truck, not bothering to wave goodbye as he drove off. He was a confusing man, but she had work to do and shrugged off his behavior before turning back to the Preacher.

"My editor has asked me to write a story about the town's new minister."

"It's like being a celebrity." He laughed.

She looked around at everyone staring. "Is there somewhere you feel comfortable talking freely?"

He noted her boots and backpack. "Let's go for a hike."

Angie loved hiking but had been too busy since the move. On the trail, she learned that Ryan met his wife at Grand Canyon University, that he'd preached in Bisbee for the last ten years and that though they'd tried, he and Elena had no children.

How the town could be unsure of him, she had no idea until he said, "My wife and I read your first book last night."

She stopped in her tracks. *So that's where the sales came from.* "Before you ask, I do believe in God, but growing up, religion left a mark on me that I'm not sure will ever go away."

"And you work it out in your novels."

She shook her head. "They're not memoirs, it's just me investigating things now that I would have been punished for even thinking about back then."

Waiting for more questions, she studied the surrounding trees and inhaled deeply. "Did you know that there's power in the scent of a pine forest that magical people believe is healing and protective."

He stunned her again by saying, "They also believe it can help with fertility, and that's part of why we're here."

She remembered the tall woman's coffee cup and worried to herself. The town would judge her books and her lifestyle as improper, but if they found out that Elena was truly magical, Angie felt the couple might be in real danger. They walked in silence for a while, and she noted that every hundred feet or so there was a cactus peeking out from underneath the pine needles. A reminder that Arizona doesn't play around and if you're going to be weak, you should probably do it somewhere else.

She'd been testing her strength since Megan came on the scene, and the prospect of going on without Jeff was already energizing her in ways that she'd never considered. Still, her resistance to the town's efforts to keep her down would be critical to the success of her new life. She would look out for her new friends, Ryan, Elena, and Doug, if Doug considered himself her friend; and she hoped they would do the same for her.

At home, she called Jeff on his mother's land line. He answered, so he hadn't been lying about that part of his trip. She wanted him to come home so they could have *the talk,* but she also felt it important that he knew how uneasy she felt, just in case.

He laughed at her. "In that tiny town, with those nice people, you should feel safer than you ever have. You're just lonely and I'll be there in a couple of days. Mom is missing me too you know."

It had only been a few days since his mother waved them out of the old house.

"You're right, Doug Farmer is very nice," she lied, "and maybe *he* would like some company."

"Doug who?"

She didn't answer him, and now that Megan had made her decision, he was worried about losing Angie too. "Angela?"

"Take your time. Love to your mom. I'll see you whenever."

"Angela!"

She hung up and opened her laptop. They had researched the housing market and the weather and even the fire danger, but they'd made a critical error by not looking up the quality of life in their new town. The former owner of the house didn't bother to mention it to them, but he vented to a northern Arizona online forum about how the church basically ran his family out after he declined to join.

He was fired from the utility company; his wife was ostracized, and his teenaged son was arrested several times for curfew violations even though he worked nights at the pharmacy.

What made Angie's blood curdle was the plea from a young man claiming to be Terrence Sullivan's partner. The former copywriter had disappeared during an accident that damaged the press. His partner believed he was murdered, but neighboring authorities said that was a conspiracy theory and refused to get involved.

There was more pounding on her door, jolting her out of her thoughts. She looked out the window and then sank down to the couch with her hands over her mouth. Were they crazy? Did mobs still come for you in the middle of the night?

"Angela Walsh!" someone yelled, "Come out here!"

She sprinted to lock the back door, but it was kicked it in as she got there. Out of nowhere, rough hands grabbed her and beat her and pulled her through the house while men and women shoved the unopened boxes to the middle of the room.

The tall woman raised two of her books in the air, shrieking, "Here! Here are the devil's own words!"

The mob tipped over the shelf, dumping the rest of her books, and poured gasoline on the pile.

They dragged her, kicking and screaming into the forest and pinned her against a pine tree. The tall woman jerked so hard on her hair that Angie thought her neck might snap.

"Your house is cursed. It invites impurities to this town, and the best way to cleanse impurity is with fire."

Had she stumbled into a cult? She felt her hands

pulled behind her and tied around the tree.

"What have I done to you?" Angie screamed.

The tall woman lifted her skirt to display the coffee burn on her ankle. "Witch!"

"No!"

Another voice from the crowd shouted, "She put a spell on Nate at the newspaper!"

Ryan and Elena pushed their way through the crowd shouting, "Stop this madness!"

Someone threw a lit branch in the house and the crowd's eyes danced as it erupted in flames. Angie's body was bruised, and blood flowed from her temples, but she lifted her head and squared her shoulders, unwilling to show them how terrified she really was.

"Preacher!" Doug Farmer approached, taking Ryan and Elena by the arms.

"Take your hands off me!" Elena cried.

"I have to get you two out of here before things get worse," Doug hissed.

Ryan jerked away. "I'm not leaving her tied to a tree."

"She's bewitching the preacher!" Several men charged at them, and Doug pushed Ryan and his wife in the truck.

He locked eyes with Angie for a moment and then slammed the door. Elena punched at him as he sped away, screaming, "We have to go back for her!"

Doug had met his wife when they were studying forestry in college and had followed her back to the town she was raised in. He had no particular interest in their religion or their rules, but he loved her desperately and when she died, he stayed to be near her grave and his precious pines. He didn't believe in their ways or participate in their *activities* but as long as he kept his head down and went to church everyone gave the grieving widower a pass. He'd grown to hate himself though, after the business with that boy, and vowed that he would never again stand by doing nothing.

"I won't let anyone else die," he said to Ryan.

"Then let us go back for her."

"That includes you."

Elena's body stilled and she stared out the window, whispering at the burning house. The mob had the local fire department standing by so that the forest didn't catch, but they hadn't expected the flames to travel in a steady stream from Angie's house to the tall woman's shed, the neighbor's hay barn, the coffee shop and the city hall. Everyone stood dumbfounded for a moment as the entire town was engulfed. Then they ran off in all directions to try to protect their property.

Alone in the shadows of the forest as the flames crept closer and closer to her tree, Angie struggled against the ropes until her body gave out. Delirious with pain and exhaustion, she slumped forward and cried.

She'd waited too long to look for her strength and she was going to pay for her laziness with her life. Using the last of her adrenaline, she writhed against the ropes once more as the fire nipped at her toes. The rope slipped the tiniest bit and by furiously twisting her body, she was able to create just enough room to get one hand free. She slapped at her ankles to douse the burning hem of her jeans, untied herself, and then ran as fast as she could down the road out of town, never looking back.

A pair of headlights pierced the darkness, growing larger as they raced toward her and, fearing it was one of the townsmen, she dove to the side of the road. The truck screeched to a halt and Doug jumped out, chasing her through the forest.

"Angie wait!"

He caught her in his arms, and she swung wildly at him with her fists, furious that he'd abandoned her to the mob and terrified that he would take her back to them.

"I was coming back for you," he panted. "Look at me." He took her face in his hands. "I was always coming back for you."

While the town smoldered in the months that followed, Jeff collected the insurance money on his new house and moved back to Phoenix at the request of his mother. Ryan and Elena transferred to a little church in Pinetop and Doug and Angie started a company to look after cabins for owners who lived in the valley.

They cleared the brush and made sure the pipes didn't freeze, and for an extra fee would have their fridges filled and their fireplaces lit when the owners came up north to visit.

Angie had even cut a deal with one man so that she could live in his cabin for two months while finishing her werewolf book. She and Doug were pulling a dead cedar tree away from his porch when he called to confirm the arrangement.

"Yes, of course," Doug heard her say, "your place is in good hands and thank you so much, Sheriff Ruiz."

She hung up grinning and Doug gave her a high five. "Are you sure this guy won't back out on you?"

"Naw, he's a deputy sheriff in some town called Chuparosa and he doesn't need the place until

November."

"Alright then."

Doug's house was spared in the fire, but he sold it to an investor from California and moved to Strawberry. His relationship with Angie was platonic, though he grew more attached to her every day. He drove away from the sheriff's cabin that night resolving to use the next two months to win her heart.

She was determined to make good use of the time as well. After waving him goodbye, she opened her laptop at the kitchen table and thought for a long time about the recent changes in her life. One change proudly showed itself at the top of her document in 14-point Times New Roman. The Werewolf's Lover, by Angie Walsh was nearly finished and was even gaining some pre-release traction on social media.

She'd also outlined a new book about a twenty first century witch burning town. The witches would never give up and the plot twist would be their superpower— fire resistance.

I've updated it a bit for the Chronicle, but this is a story I wrote before Chuparosa had fully come to life. My son used to work for a grocery store and part of it is taken directly from events that occurred during one of his late-night shifts. Fortunately, in real life the woman survived but, you know how I am.

Oliver's Origin Story

The last hour of Boone's shift was spent in the parking lot, hauling carts.

"At least it's only 112 degrees today," he muttered to himself.

The Arizona summer hadn't been taken into consideration when he applied to the grocery store at Christmastime. *Epic fail.* Noting the time, he shoved a train into the corral, untied his apron and rushed to clock out. Judy had made him promise to come straight home so he could see her off.

His mother was going to spend the weekend with her coven, The Desert Doves. Apparently, they were hell bent on getting revenge on the guy who tried to kidnap Sonia Trainer's daughter, Missy. Missy was a couple of years older than Boone and would have never talked to the likes of him about her ordeal, but he'd heard that she was leaving town for a few days to *get some rest*. In the meantime, the Doves would be cooking up a hex so vile that Boone shuddered to think about it.

The air conditioning in his hand-me-down Corolla never really kicked in, so he was drenched with sweat when he got home. Inside the door of their tiny house, his senses were assaulted by the eighties, courtesy of Duran Duran. He grabbed a sports drink from the refrigerator and found Judy pulling items from her closet and dancing them over to the open suitcase on the bed. She picked the little black cat out of the suitcase, set him on the bed, and returned to the closet while the cat jumped back in the suitcase. Boone stood at the door watching them cheerfully repeat the asinine routine for as long as he could stand it, then he took her phone and closed the music app.

"Hey!" Her annoyance turned to concern at his flushed appearance and she snatched a spray bottle from the top of her dresser. "Here, spritz this on your face and you'll feel better in no time."

He waved her off. "Keep your mad sorcery away from me, woman."

She studied him for a long moment. "Are you sure you're going to be okay this weekend?"

"I'm nineteen years old. Besides, you're the one going on a three-day bender." He tossed the cat to the floor, and it jumped back on the bed. "Also, I have your familiar to watch over me."

"Boone, I'm experiencing a spiritual awakening—didn't you read that book I gave you?"

"No."

"Speaking of Oliver," she picked up the cat and gave him a squeeze. "Don't forget about him. He's very sensitive. I sent you a link to his favorite YouTube video, the one with the birds in the forest. He also likes to watch Tom and Jerry cartoons."

Her suitcase was way too full so he gently moved her out of the way and leaned on it with all of his weight so she could zip it up.

"Just call me Judy Jetsetter!"

"I'm not gonna do that."

Her phone beeped with a new text. "Molly's here! I ordered you a pizza and it's on the way."

He dragged her suitcase down the front steps and heaved it in the trunk of Molly's car.

"Hi Boone! You're so handsome, I just don't understand why the girls aren't crawling all over you."

"These are dark times."

Judy took his arm. "Listen, make sure you call me, and you better respond to my texts. I will send Sheriff Scott if you don't."

"Will you just go?" He checked his attitude, and added, "I love you Mom, and I want you to have a good time."

Inside, he closed the door and leaned against it. Alone, at last—sort of.

Oliver stared up at him hopefully. "Meow?"

Full of pizza and empowered with temporary independence, Boone brought his laptop to the couch and logged on to his English class. He hated English, but hated the grocery store even more, so was dutifully completing the prerequisites for a certificate in heating and air conditioning repair. He'd made it through high school without getting shot to death just in time for the world to be infected with the Coronavirus. With the vaccine finally available, it appeared that the earth was going to spin on for a while so he would have to work to survive.

As the planet boiled, especially in a state like Arizona, Boone figured a career in HVAC would make him rich, or at least financially stable enough to survive the first wave of societal breakdown. While he daydreamed of becoming a real-life John Connor, Oliver hopped up and walked across his keyboard.

"Get off!" He shoved the cat away, but it stuck it's face in the camera startling Boone's friend Leo who had just entered the Discord.

"Meow?"

"Holy crap!"

"Sorry Leo, hang on. I've got to get his video going." Boone scooped up the ancient tablet Judy passed down to the cat and navigated to YouTube.

"What cartoon did she say you liked?"

Oliver blinked at him. "Meow."

Boone started an episode of Rick and Morty and positioned the tablet on the floor next to the couch. Oliver looked from the tablet to Boone suspiciously but settled down to watch.

"Bruh, your cat has his own tablet?"

"His life is way better than mine."

Boone managed to get his essay turned in just before the midnight deadline. Since he opened the store that morning, the scheduling gods naturally decided to have him close the next day. He took a second to wish a pox on them, but also a moment of gratitude for the hours he could sleep in.

Judy worked from home and Oliver wasn't used to being left alone so he panicked when Boone went to the bathroom to get ready for bed. After trying unsuccessfully to slide himself under the door, he managed to reach the bathmat with his paw. It bunched up at the jamb and wouldn't come through the opening, no matter how many times he pulled it against the door.

When his claw got stuck in the fibers, his panic grew into hysteria, and he threw his body at the door.

Slam. "Meeeeeooow!" Slam. "Meeeeeeoow!"

Boone jerked the door open and Oliver, still attached to the bathmat, slid across the bathroom floor with it.

"Je-sus Christ!"

Once rescued and satisfied that all was well, Oliver sauntered away, leaving Boone standing stupidly in the hallway, bathmat in hand.

At 3am, Oliver's tiny soul felt a familiar tug toward the joyful, random nighttime activities he so loved. Unsure of where to begin, he darted frenetically from one end of the house to the other, along the back of the couch, into the mini blinds and on top of the bookcase. There, he stopped briefly to survey his dark kingdom, and instantly spotted a wolf spider making its way up the leg of a bar stool near the kitchen island. Narrowing his focus, he crouched, shook his tail end a few times, and made the jump.

As he landed, his furry body skidded across the slippery wood floors, Tokyo drifting into the bar stool.

It dominoed its neighbor, crashing both stools into a pile.

Boone sat bolt upright. Oliver's frenzied lurches and scratches as the spider evaded capture echoed through the otherwise silent house. He stomped down the hall, flipped on the kitchen light and surveyed the toppled stools and Judy's marred wood floor.

"Are you kidding me?"

"Meow."

Later that morning, Judy texted a picture of her and the other Doves from somewhere in the desert, surrounded by candles and wine bottles.

> J: Miss you! (witch emoji; red heart emoji)
>   What are you up to?
> B: *Picture of the Joker*
> J: How's Ollie? (Black cat emoji; black heart
>   emoji)
> B: *Picture of the cat from Pet Cemetery*
> J: (eye roll emoji)

Bonk. As he left for work, Boone hadn't noticed the cat sitting there and opened the front door into his head.

Oliver shook it off and stared up at him. "Meow?"

Boone sighed and grabbed the tablet. He propped it up against a pillow on the couch and found the link Judy sent him.

"The video is supposed to run for eight hours, but I forgot to charge this up, so you might be screwed."

Oliver began swatting at the birds in the forest, so Boone shook his head and trudged off to work.

At midnight, Michael, the cashier, nudged his arm and gestured at a very obviously drunk woman wobbling down the aisle toward their register.

"Hey Boone, is that your girlfriend?"

"That's never been funny. Ever."

She stumbled and swayed and dumped an armload of mini wine boxes on the conveyer belt.

"Make sure you card me sweetie," she slurred, "I could be a minor."

Boone and Michael looked at each other. In no universe was she a minor.

While digging in her purse she stopped suddenly and looked right at Boone. His eyes grew wide, and he took several steps back. She bent over, put her hands on her knees, arched her back, and hurled. Michael jumped on the counter as what seemed like a gallon of barf splashed on the floor.

She raised her head and Boone dove out of the way as she sent a projectile stream where he had been standing. Her eyes rolled up, her head fell back, and then her body hit the floor as if she were a plank of wood.

"Holy shit!" Boone stared in disbelief for a moment and then realized she wasn't moving.

He yelled for the security guard and turned to Michael. "Call 9-1-1!"

He tiptoed through the vomit and used the toe of his boot to turn her head so she wouldn't choke. When sirens could be heard in the parking lot, he gathered the wine boxes from the conveyer belt.

Michael stared at him. "What are you doing?"

"Go-backs, I guess."

In all the excitement, no one noticed the large green

orb of light that followed Boone to the liquor department.

A monsoon storm had been brewing all day and a wall of dust hit Boone in the face as he left the store, and enormous rain drops pelted him all the way to his car. His windshield wipers scratched across the glass like a screaming banshee and he was so busy trying to get the defrost to work that he never saw the green orb sneak in the backseat just before he slammed the door.

At home in the kitchen, he found cheerios scattered across the entire floor and Oliver stuck inside their plastic container on the kitchen counter. The cat treats sat unbothered in an identical container next to where the cereal had been stored.

After being released, Oliver began to intently watch the green light that had slipped inside behind Boone. He leapt at it as it traveled through the house.

Boone looked up from sweeping the cereal and said, "Why are you like this?"

In the shower, Boone heard a bang against the door. Then, another one, and another one. With shampoo dripping in his eyes, he wrapped a towel around his waist and flung the door open to yell at the cat, but Oliver wasn't there. He dripped down the hall to find him pooping in the litter box.

"Meow?"

Later, he and Leo were playing a video game online when Boone's bedroom door slammed loud enough for both boys to jump.

Oliver looked up from Rick and Morty. "Meow?"

Boone knew he should do some homework on his day off, but it had been a weird week, so he decided to do nothing instead. He was poking around for a snack when another text came in from his mother.

```
J: Have you checked the mail?
B: no
J: Take Ollie with you
B: no
J: DO IT (angry face emoji)
B: fine
```

Oliver jumped around grabbing at the leash as Boone lifted the little harness from a hook by the door.

"Hold still." He said, struggling to strap him in.

He had one foot caught under the mesh, but Oliver hobble hopped down the steps until Boone noticed.

"Oh, my god."

"Meow."

He fixed the harness and they continued on to the mailbox where a text came in from Michael.

```
M: dude that drunk lady from last night DIED
B: no way
M: (dead smiley emoji)
```

After gathering the mail, Boone stopped short at the front door and exchanged looks with Oliver. The living room area rug was scrunched into a wad against the television stand.

"Meow."

He tossed his mom's mail on her bed, unharnessed

the cat, and went to the kitchen where he stopped short again. The refrigerator door was open. The doors on the oven, microwave and dishwasher were open as well, and the green orb of light hovered over lit burners on the stove. Oliver hissed and arched his back.

An hour later, Leo stood in the kitchen with Boone. The green orb was floating over the toaster near where Oliver stood on the counter keeping watch.

Leo patted Oliver on the head. "Good job, bud."

"Meow."

Turning to Boone, he added, "Dude, it's cold over here." He blew at the small appliance. "Look, I can see my breath."

Boone stuffed his hands in his pockets. "It can't be a ghost. Judy's crazy rituals are specifically designed to keep this kind of shit out of the house."

"Maybe it snuck in after she left."

"From where? I only go to work and back."

They blinked at each other, and Boone sighed, "Oh no. The drunk lady."

After scanning the internet for ghost removal techniques, they searched Judy's room for her sage wands.

"Got em!" Boone announced, holding up a bundle for each of them.

Leo pulled a large leather-bound book from underneath Judy's bed. "What's this?"

"That's her book of crazy."

Leo flipped through the pages. "This is actually pretty cool. It says here we need salt too."

"What?"

"Your mom is an interesting lady."

The green orb seemed agitated when they lit the sage bundles, and Oliver pounced alongside as it zigzagged through the house.

"Should we say something?" Boone wondered.

Leo shook his sage at the orb and shouted, "Get out!"

"Right, that should do it."

The living room filled with smoke and Oliver began to sneeze, but as Boone moved to open the front door, the orb vibrated wildly and the air warmed throughout the house.

"It's working!"

The boys jumped around with excitement until they were suddenly gagging, overcome by the stench of wine barf. The orb tipped a vase of plastic flowers from a table in the entryway, but its light had dimmed to the palest of greens as it hovered waist high in front of Boone. He stepped over the shards of glass and waved his sage wand again. The orb darted toward the open door followed by Oliver who chased it all the way outside.

Boone flicked Oliver's ear as he sniffed at the salt they poured along the threshold of every door, at every windowsill and in a circle around the couch. "Don't eat that, dumb ass."

When Leo was gone and Boone finally settled in with his laptop, Oliver jumped on the keyboard, but that time Boone scratched him between the ears.

"How are we going to tell Judy about all of this?"

"Meow?"

Boone looked warily around the living room. He'd turned on every light in the house, but it wasn't much comfort, so he made a mental list of all the questions he would ask his mother. Oliver seemed to sense his unease and curled up in his lap while they watched Rick and Morty and waited for her to get home.

***Dedicated to Shadow, the best kitty in the house.
Rest in peace: February 2024***

The Watching Thing

It was a subtle move. In fact, he almost missed it. The imperceptible glance over her shoulder was so practiced that it was almost involuntary after all those years. Mena Ruiz had a secret and, though he didn't yet know the whole of it, Thomas was delighted to have found her out.

He'd caught sight of it when her daughter Christina released Tromluí at the birthday party. Tromluí had whirled through the crowd looking for a target and when it brushed against the cowboy, Mena recognized it as a spirit and compared it to her own. She wasn't tall and strong like Thomas's daughters, and he wondered how long she'd carried the weight of the thing on her tiny frame. Her eyes shone with the fierceness of a survivor but drooped slightly from the mental toll that survival extracted. She'd gotten remarkably adept at keeping her secret and Thomas was fascinated by her.

He was surprised that Daniel hadn't noticed but, then again, Mena was not Daniel's concern. Thomas would not have been concerned either, except that she was Laura's friend. If something happened to Mena, Laura would not be at her best and he needed Laura at her best.

Hidden, he watched for several weeks as Earth's Defenses had recovered from their battles with Fiona and the troll. They tried to reduce their experience to clever stories over drinks around a firepit in the cowboy's back yard, but the ordeal had changed them. There would be no more naïveté, carelessness or miscommunication and they were bonded closer than ever.

As their injuries healed and their strength returned, Mena did not relax. While remaining physically close to the others, Thomas noted that mentally she was sitting just outside of the group's collective rebound which, he worried, would make her a liability in the months to come. He followed her closely and one night, while watching through the bathroom window as she prepared for bed, her spirit made an appearance.

Mena stepped into a pair of cotton pajama shorts after her shower and picked up the top, but then sighed and laid it down on the counter. Twisting her body between the vanity mirror and the mirror on the closet door, she examined her back. Thomas leaned closer and saw her wet hair flutter as the skin rippled underneath it. She faced the shower curtain, pretending to be unbothered as the creature slithered along her back.

It pushed against her hips and shoulders, demanding attention until finally, attached at her waist like a conjoined twin, it materialized and gave her hair a sharp tug.

Her breathing quickened but, curiously, she ignored it and bent to splash her face with water. When she stood, the thing slashed at her, leaving a bloody scratch across her cheek. She turned away and it took her by the chin, forcing her gaze back to the mirror.

Continuing the battle of wills, she squeezed her eyes closed, but it bit down on her shoulder until she yelped and pounded her fist on the counter. Then, what Thomas imagined was an all too familiar look of resignation settled over her face.

Pleased with its success, the spirit wrapped her in its arms and slid its fingers around her neck. For a moment, Thomas thought it was going to choke her to death and he moved to intervene, but it whispered something in her ear then dissolved into a mist that settled around her body.

She hastily put on her top and left the bathroom, so he sat perched atop the fence for a while, lost in thought. He knew she was alone and was weighing the merits of barging into the house for answers when she lurched out of the shadows, hissing, "Leave me alone, demon."

"I think you know the difference between me and a demon." His eyes blackened. "It's truer to say that you're the one with a demon. Isn't it?"

She lifted her chin. "It's attached to me, so it won't

help you. You can't use it against Laura."

It must have told her he was outside. "I don't want to use it against Laura. In fact, I may be able to help you get rid of it."

She felt the spirit bounce across her nerves with a warning, but the prospect of being free of it was so tempting that she had to force herself to refuse. "I don't trust you."

"That's because you're not stupid." She had no particular powers that Thomas was aware of, other than a smart mouth and a big heart. But, like everyone in Chuparosa, Mena Ruiz had a story and he wanted to hear it.

"I know your husband and the cowboy are dealing with a rollover out on Yuma Road, so we've got plenty of time to chat."

She folded her arms and turned away from him, not believing he could help her, or that he wanted to. But if Thomas could see it, he could be willing to answer some of her questions.

For too long, she'd been confused and afraid—even ashamed of the thing that had invaded her life so many years ago. Though the creature twisted her insides in protest, she felt no small amount of relief to talk about it with someone else who could understand. Even someone like Thomas.

She kept her back to him and said softly, "Laura calls it the Watching Thing."

So, Laura knows about it too. Of course she does. 'Show me where you got it."

"I can't show you." She faced him again, eyes flashing in the moonlight. "I burned the place down."

"Then tell me."

She had burned it down, but looking into the darkness that night, she could see the house in her mind as clearly as if she'd taken Thomas thirty-five years back in time.

In 1988, Mena Marquez played varsity volleyball for Chuparosa High School and her boyfriend, Chuck Ruiz, never missed a game. He took her home afterward and they would make out in his truck, parked in the desert at the end of the street.

Since she was too embarrassed to invite him in, a decade would pass before he would see the inside of her house, and it would be charred and smoldering by then.

Mena's father, George, was a hoarder, obsessed with yard sale fixer uppers. He bought broken things and then bought magazines about how to fix them and never touched the projects again. He never managed to fix anything else around the house either which, by the time she was a teenager, was in shambles.

George flew into a violent rage when her mother, Carla, tried to clean up or call for repairs, which added more and more to the piles of broken things. There wasn't a widely known name for his disorder at the time, and when Carla could no longer handle the shame and the damage, she divorced him for a man at the Sheriff's Department who the high school kids called Deputy Dickhead.

Already showing signs of her father's disorder, Mena's older sister had left home the year before in a Ford Pinto loaded down with so much stuff that she could barely see over the dashboard. Carla feared Mena would have it too and refused to let her move into the house she shared with the Deputy. Mena's bedroom, though, was the only room in which one could see the floor.

When Carla and the Deputy got married, George slipped into a depressive episode from which he never recovered. Though she tried on occasion to secretly work through the dirty dishes or the laundry piles, there was nowhere to store the clean ones.

Eventually, Mena gave up and focused on keeping her room spotless and her homework done, counting down the days until graduation. She worked at the YMCA after school and most nights ate dinner with Chuck's or Laura's families.

Laura's mother was cruel to her own children, but Brona could be quite charitable to everyone else and, as graduation neared, Mena was able to sleep over most nights with the Deanes.

It was during the months before Brona's kindness that Mena considered the darkest days of her life. After work, she picked her way through piles of magazines and boxes full of yard sale junk that was somehow always damp and covered in piles of laundry. From a near lifeless body buried somewhere on the couch, she would hear, "Don't touch my stuff."

In her closet, she kept a small collection of household items that were clean and safe for her to use. One night after a game, Mena selected a towel from her stash and made her way to the bathroom, the room she hated the most. For weeks she'd been able to shower at school or at work, but that night, she was stuck at home.

The junk piled in the sink reached halfway up the mirror, but it was unusable anyway as the faucet had been broken for years. George had once dug up the tile in an angry fit after Carla complained about the state of the room, so the floor remained bare concrete and glue.

Hard water stained the toilet bowl and the tank cover leaned against the wall because the valve was broken and they had to jiggle things around to make it flush.

She pulled back the dirty shower curtain and winced at the grout between the yellow tiles which was black with mold. The wall around the faucet had caved in when she was little and George duct taped a black trash bag around the fixtures. The tape had since peeled back leaving the bag hanging loose in several places, exposing a wet, dark passage into the walls of the house.

The shower head was corroded so she plugged the drain to fill the tub for a bath. She washed herself quickly, keeping her head down until a breeze drifted over her from behind the plastic. When she looked up, a long Pinacate Beetle crawled around the bag and onto the side of the tub. She screeched and pushed back, sloshing water everywhere and unsettling the beetle that then fell in the water with her. As she scrambled to get away from it, a hand reached around the plastic bag, scooped up the beetle and tossed it on the concrete floor.

Mena fell back in the water, gaping as the thing slunk out of the wall. It was pale and long, hairless with large black eyes and a gangly neck. It smelled of mint, which overpowered the scent of mold she had grown so accustomed to. She drew her knees to her chest, barely breathing as it rested an elbow on the soap holder.

She was frozen in terror, but it simply watched her until she began to shiver as the water turned cold. It then worked its way behind her, and she felt its hands on her bare shoulders. It stretched its neck around to look her in the face and she stared into its black eyes for what seemed like hours, unable to scream and convinced that she was going to die.

When it finally blinked at her, she passed out from the shock and woke up draped over the side of the tub. Though she could no longer see it, from that day forward, she could feel the creature inside of her.

"Laura tried to banish it for me once, but the spell didn't work." Mena leaned against the fence and sighed. "It watches and waits until things are awful and then it shows up and makes them worse. I nearly died in childbirth because of it. It's like it feeds on the chaos of life."

"I don't think so." Thomas steepled his fingers under his chin and thought for a while. "Does Chuck know?"

"I don't keep things from my husband." She made a face. "Well, not many things. It was there the first night we..." She abandoned that sentence, allowing her voice to trail off.

Thomas looked up. "The night you lost your virginity to him. You must have been so nervous." He was thoughtful for a minute more and then clapped his hands. "This spirit is not evil, and it's something we can use."

She moved away from him. "You're insane."

"Mena, Mena, Mena. For all those years, you have misunderstood your gift."

She lifted her head and held his gaze, determined

not to let him play with her. "The Watching Thing is a curse and only you would believe otherwise."

He took her by the arm, and she would have pulled away but for the flicker of compassion behind his eyes when he said, "I'll have it explained by someone you trust."

A knock on the door in the middle of night would be alarming to anyone, but Drew Clarke's crushing sense of panic was based on plenty of experience. Tumbling out of bed, he sprinted through the house to push his eye against the peephole.

Still in her pajamas, Mena Ruiz stood on his welcome mat looking remarkably calm considering that Thomas towered behind her with his hands on her shoulders. Drew threw open the door and pulled her close to him, glaring at Thomas.

"What have you done to her?"

"Oh, will you relax?" Thomas pushed past them, made his way to the kitchen and called over his shoulder, "I need you to help me prove a point."

Mena looked up at him and nodded. "You're going to think I'm crazy."

"Not likely." Drew narrowed his eyes at Thomas, who motioned them to the kitchen table and pulled open the refrigerator door.

"Hurry up and tell him because we haven't got all night." Thomas rooted around, finding ketchup, two sticks of butter and four bottles that remained from a six pack of Coors Light. "You live like this?"

"If you're hungry, check the freezer."

Indeed, Drew had piles of frozen meals and two

pints of mint chocolate chip ice cream. Thomas rattled a box of rock-solid ravioli chunks at him. "This is pathetic."

Ignoring him, Drew filled a pot of water for coffee and then gave Mena his full attention. His cat, Daphne, poked her head out from the bedroom with a judgmental scowl. She'd had Drew's legs pinned in her favorite position as they slept and couldn't believe the nerve of the intruders. Daphne was familiar with the woman though and jumped in her lap.

At one point in Mena's story, while she navigated some random input from Thomas, Drew rose to scour his bookshelves and, once again, there was a knock at the door. Mena knew that Laura could sense when the people she loved were suffering and was not at all surprised when Drew ushered her and Watson to the kitchen.

Normally, Daphne would not be caught dead in the same room with Watson, as she was offended by his very existence. But she was comfortable in Mena's lap and settled for a half-hearted swipe at the German Shepherd's nose.

Laura's stony gaze swept around the room and settled on Thomas. He shoveled the last of the ravioli in his mouth and raised his hands. "I am just trying to help."

Drew brought Laura's attention to a psychology book and laid it open on the table. "It gives me actual heartburn to say it, but I think Thomas is right about this Watching Thing."

Thomas smiled to himself and poured a cup of coffee. He'd known the Preacher would do anything to help Mena, even if it did cause him pain.

Laura raised an eyebrow. "Go on."

"Mena, does it speak to you?"

The women shared a sideways glance. It was clear that they were reluctant to tell the whole story, so Drew was careful when he pressed. "What made you decide to burn down the house?"

Thomas leaned in, anxious to see how much she was willing to reveal.

Laura took Mena's hands in hers. "We're safe here." She gave Thomas a warning look. "But it's up to you."

"I guess it doesn't really matter anymore." Mena shrugged her shoulders and continued, "After two miscarriages, I'd just had Tina and it was a horrible experience. Then my father died and I..." Her voice faltered, "I had to do something about the house."

Laura remembered very clearly how they had tried. Chuck was gone a lot for work in those days, so she, Mena and Cara decided to tackle the cleanup on their own. The coroner warned them that it was bad, but there was no way they could have prepared for what they encountered.

It was revolting. They'd brought cleaning supplies and a whole box of trash bags, but the dark, oppressive energy of the place nearly knocked them down at the doorway. They could barely breathe from the stench and though they stayed on the narrow path made by the paramedics, rats and insects of all kinds scuttled around them.

They'd turned in panicked circles, overwhelmed by the task at hand and the sadness that hung in the air. It was then that the Watching Thing reached around and covered Mena's eyes. The room began to shake and, as garbage toppled around them, a stick lighter fell at

Laura's feet.

When the ground settled, she picked it up and flicked it at the spirit. Remarkably, it let go of Mena's eyes and she took the lighter from Laura, asking, "How much trouble do you think I'll get into if I just burn it to the ground?"

Laura pulled the flame into her palms and said, "What if they can't prove you did it?" The Watching Thing pulled excitedly at Mena's hair and shoulders, and she and Cara moved trash away from the walls so that Laura could shoot streams of flame into the electrical outlets.

"The place went up so fast that we almost didn't get out." Mena said.

Drew sat back in his chair, once again amazed by the strength of the women in his life. "Laura was on the right track when she named it," he explained, "because that's exactly what it does. It watches out for you."

Laura and Mena crossed their arms, unconvinced.

"It showed up during the worst time in your life and if you think back, I'll bet you can point to more events it helped you survive. I don't believe it was blinding your eyes that day in the house, I believe it was shielding them."

"Hear me out: sometimes people dissociate when they go through traumatic events, especially children. When that happens, something in the subconscious takes over and helps them cope by reframing the experience as a dream or an alternate reality. But you live in Chuparosa and, however unsettling the end result may be, Chuparosa will always find a way to take care of its own."

It was not in Mena's nature, so she had not cried in

a very long time, but her body suddenly shook with sobs. Laura pulled her close and smoothed her long dark hair.

"If he's right, it's back now because we're part of Daniel's Defenses and it's trying to keep you safe." She gave Thomas another look. "Tonight, it could have been warning you of danger."

"It probably lays dormant until something happens," Drew agreed, "until its needed."

Laura held her friend tighter and gave him a pleading look. "We're going to need more help with this."

Drew was already mentally planning a call to David Trainer. David and his family lived in town, and he worked as a mental health counselor for the state of Arizona. Drew had long hoped they could somehow collaborate, given the need in Chuparosa.

"You can't get rid of it, so you might as well use it to your advantage," Thomas offered.

"Ever the opportunist," Laura criticized, but privately agreed, and she would discuss that with Mena at a later time.

After yet another knock on the door Drew ushered in a pair of tired Sheriff's deputies. On their way back from the car accident, they'd noticed the women's vehicles in Drew's driveway.

"Baby, what the hell is going on?" Keeping his eyes on Thomas, Bash reached down to pet Daphne. She'd had all the socializing she could bear for one night though, and scampered underneath Drew's bed.

Laura whirled on Thomas. "I swear to God if you caused that car crash, just to—"

"Save your indignation for a more appropriate time,

dearest." Thomas stood to leave. "I've eased Mena's mind and offered you all a source of untapped power which you will very likely need in the coming months." He bent forward in a dramatic bow. "You're welcome."

She realized that until then he had, quite uncharacteristically, said almost nothing throughout the night.

"Why are you doing this?"

"Because I can."

"Helping her changes nothing between us."

"Doesn't it though?" He scrunched his nose at her. "Just a little?"

Later as he peeked through the window from outside, Thomas felt a slight tug on his heart. The others gathered around Mena with their support and even before his *punishment*, that was an experience he'd never shared with his brothers. He envied how humans came together for the ones they loved. He had envisioned his children as sources of power from which he could draw, and that had turned out to be the case, but not at all in the way he intended.

About the Author

Vanessa Haney grew up in rural Arizona with, tragically, no access to the Other Side. Had there been a portal, she would have gone through it a long time ago. Instead, she makes a happy life in less rural Arizona with her son Connor, her partner Mike and a black cat named Felix. There she writes, hikes and watches way too many horror movies.

Sign up to follow her adventures at:
http://www.vanessahaneywrites.com

158

www.ingramcontent.com/pod-product-compliance
Lightning Source LLC
Chambersburg PA
CBHW060327310726
48976CB00007B/2478